# WALDIN'S WISH

**Enchanted Immortals**
**Book 1**

## F.G. Adams

Cover Design:
LJ Anderson with Mayhem Creations

Interior Design & Formatting:
Daryl Banner

Edited by:
Daryl Banner

*Dedicated to our grandma,*

*for encouraging us to be who we are today.*

*We miss you and will love you always.*

# LIST OF CHAPTERS

# WALDIN'S WISH

**Enchanted Immortals**
**Book 1**

# PROLOGUE

## *Peru, South America*

In the bowels of the great mountain Huayna Picchu in Peru, the cool moist air drifts heavily throughout the intricately woven caves of blackness, a never-ending labyrinth with a stale stench of death permeating from the slight air flow seeping through the tunnels. Walls of slippery, wet rocks with sharp, jagged edges from centuries of mineral deposits and eons of erosion continue the maze. Lifeless.

In the underground makeshift tomb well below the Inca ceremonial Moon Temple, a figure stands hunched over, waiting. Muted light filters throughout the grotto from the two lit torches perched at the entrance. Decay seeps from the exposed skin of the man. No, not man—*monster*. Flesh rots away from the bone, piece by piece, like a dead animal left in the woods for weeks.

1

A sizable obsidian stone hangs from the ceiling in the center of the room, angling down toward the solitary rock-sculpted altar. The black gem is called the Abgrund Stone, better known as the Infinite Abyss which holds all the Night Realm power.

"திறந்த எள்" *Open sesame*, the man whispers into the subterranean tomb.

The lone figure turns his head to the entrance as a bright light flashes, and the sound of heavy footsteps rumble through the cavern. He watches as a huge, shadowed frame steps into the cave burdened by a large bundle over his shoulders.

"Did you retrieve what I desired, Jafar?" the decaying man croaks from the middle of the cave.

"Yes, Your Majesty." The figure bows while balancing the heavy load.

Walking over to his master, the man lays the massive bundle carefully out across the stone table set in the center of the room, mindful of his actions.

"It is just as you wished, Your Majesty. He is thirty-five human years old. A Vampire youngling. He's been turned for only ten years." Jafar looks eagerly to the rotting man, expectant and hopeful.

The dark cloak is pulled back to reveal a strikingly handsome specimen. Long black locks surround a narrow face. The Vampire's tan color and high cheekbones give away his Indian heritage.

"Ah, Jafar. You have done very well this time."

Jafar bows again, then reaches inside his pocket to retrieve a tattered black and white photo. "I found this on your new body, Your Majesty. It bears a striking resemblance to Maarku."

A decrepit hand reaches out to snag the photograph. Peering at the tattered paper from deteriorating eyes, the man studies the picture. Two men are standing side by side, one with his arm draped over the other, his gaze showing a look of fatherly admiration and warmth toward him. As he examines it closer, a sinister smile spreads across his face.

"Yes. Yes. I believe you are correct, my old friend. This is most certainly him."

Evil laughter erupts from the crumpled remains of the man, pinging off the walls, echoing through the cavernous space. Soon Jafar joins in.

"We finally have him, Jafar. And I now know his weakness. Come. We must begin the ritual immediately. We have much to do and little time to do it in."

They prepare the body lying on the stone table. After stripping him naked, they cuff his hands and feet. Jafar scurries around prepping while the man leans laboriously against the table. When all is ready, the ceremony begins. With shallow breaths, he commences with reciting the incantation:

"ஓ இருள் அதிகாரம் நான் உம்மை வேண்டிக்கொள்ளுகிறேன். நான் கடவுள் Zenon மற்றும் அம்மன் அகஸ்டா சக்தி அழைப்பு விடுக்கிறோம். டார்க் நைட் அதிகாரம் வெளியிட. இருண்ட ஆன்மா பள்ளத்தை நரகத்தில், Abgrund ஸ்டோன் உள்ள இருக்கும். என்னை மாற்றம் சக்தி தாருங்கள். அவரது உடல் ஆன்மா, உடல் ஆன்மா மாற்றம், என்னுடைய."

*("Oh power of darkness, I beseech thee. I call upon the power of the god Zenon and goddess Augusta. Release the power of the dark knight. The dark souls existing within the hell of abyss, the Abgrund Stone. Grant me the power of transformation. Transferring soul for soul, body for body, his for mine.")*

4

# CHAPTER 1

**New York City, Spring of 1820**

*Aldin*

As I walk home in the early evening light, the wind whips through my hair from the salty coastal waters causing a tornado affect around me and making me shiver. I bundle my coat closer and wrap my tattered scarf more firmly around my neck. There's a slight chill in the air that is reminiscent of the harsh winter. But the air has changed, becoming more crisp, and with it brings a new hope for better days. The sun slowly sets off to the west as I buckle my coat tighter.

I worked a long day at the shipyard. My body is taut and aching from the overworked, underpaid conditions I'm forced to endure. It's the only job I can find or the only legitimate job I can get. I'm a street rat after all, scouring around to find any decent work. My father passed away a few years

5

ago and that left me in charge of the family. My mother, God bless her, cooks and cleans for a rich family uptown, but it's still not enough. My baby sister needs to go to school—just another thing we can't afford.

I'm only eighteen years old. Old enough to be a man, yet still naïve enough to not know what being a man entails. Don't get me wrong; I can handle myself, being bigger than most and having an attitude to boot. I just never thought I would be in this position. Who ever would?

Picking up my pace, I watch the lonely streets ahead of me. Grey shadows and odd sounds echo throughout them. A few more blocks and I'll be home, our modest spot in this enormous land. The apartment is a small flat that has one bedroom and a communal bath. It's all we can afford on the sparse income mama and I get. We had to move to the city after dad died. It was rough leaving behind the family farm, but mouths needed feeding, and without livestock or money, we had no choice.

Reaching the last block, I tense as a dark figure moves out from the alley. The hairs on the back of my neck stand on end as I move away from the giant figure approaching, trying to dart around him.

A deep baritone voice with a hint of a foreign accent reaches out to me. "Hello, boy."

Since I'm the only one on the street other than this hackle-raising man, I stop in my tracks. Turning around slowly, I face the pursuer waiting for me.

He speaks again. "How would you like to earn some extra coins?" The hypnotic timbre of the voice envelopes me, seeming to trap me in place. It has a calming effect, actually.

My face betrays me. I'm excited by the prospect of earning more money, yet at the same time leery of this shadowed alley man. I take a moment to look him over. Donning a pair of expensive boots with tassels hanging off the sides, the incandescent gas mantle from the streetlamp plays across his nondescript features. He's impeccably dressed with a dark hooded cloak that masks his face, obscuring his features, and I can only spot his eyes which seem to glow. Those eyes give me pause as I catch a flicker of red playing around his pupils—there one minute, gone the next.

My pulse quickens as I take a few awkward steps back in retreat of this threatening being, trying to decide if what I see is real or just a play on the dimly lit murkiness around me.

Again, the voice snares me and says, "What do you say, boy? If you could have three wishes, what would they be?"

I'm shocked, unable to answer. No one has ever asked me what I wanted. Sure, I've dreamed of better days, better things, but I know my life; thinking of such things is a pipe dream. My mind races to a time when I didn't carry the burden I do now, full of aspirations I wanted out of my life ... all before my father died.

"I'm not sure, really. What do you mean, sir?"

"Well, it's really rather simple. If you could have three wishes, anything at all that you wanted the most ... what would you wish for?"

The silky baritone voice envelopes my senses while sending pimpled flesh over my arms, reminding me of the predatory nature this being represents. But I'm hooked and answer as my overworked brain complies with his question.

"I would have lots of money, for starters, so that my mother and sister Ana were taken care of." I give a sly smile, compelled to continue with my next wish. "I would also have lots of women at my beck and call." I hear the man chuckle a little as I'm giving into my wishes. "Then, of course, I'd want to live forever!"

"Yes, of course you would," exclaims the man. "What if I told you that I could grant your three wishes and change your life forever?"

This is incredible, but doubtful at best. I can't even imagine this man could do anything of the sort. He would need magic or something, and I don't believe in such things. I gaze at the lone figure who has somehow shifted closer into my personal space without me knowing.

"What's your name, boy?" the man asks as he extends his hand to me. "I am Lord Marcus Dalca."

"Aldin, sir. Aldin Kovac," I say as I reach out to grasp his hand.

An immediate surge of electrical pulses race through my arm from this man's touch. I try to pull back, but his grip is sure and I can't get loose. Sudden panic floods my system and my eyes round with fright.

The man coolly speaks again. "I can give you everything your heart desires, Aldin. All you have to do is agree."

That sweet rich bass flows through our connection, giving me peace. *Can this be real? Am I dreaming?* My heart pounds loudly within my chest while my breathing becomes uneven from the anxiety of the prospect.

"What do you want from me?" I ask, whispering, still clasping his much larger hand with mine.

"Nothing much. Just agree to become part of my ranks, if you will. Work for me and all of your dreams, desires, and wishes will come true," he states in a formal manner that exudes wealth and privilege.

I nod my head because this is just so unbelievable that I can't wait another second.

Marcus continues to say, "I must hear you say the words, Aldin. You have to tell me you agree … with your words."

Such a strange request from this intimidating man. It's as if he's asking permission. For what? Clearing my throat, I take a deep breath. "Yes, I will work for you in order to attain my wishes and desires."

I instantly feel the change in the air, a power that sizzles, engulfing us both. Swaddling around us, caressing, squeezing, and consuming. Marcus leans in, hand still tightly grasping mine, and that's when I see them. His eyes are flaming red and sprouting from his upturned smiling lips are long sharp … fangs.

*NO!* I scream through my head, wishing the cry to burst from my mouth, but it's too late. Plunged into darkness, I know no more and my world is over.

# CHAPTER 2

**Boston, Massachusetts 2010**
**Harvard University**

*Wren*

The insistent music of Black Eyed Peas singing *I've Got a Feeling* rings loudly in my ears. It causes me to stir, along with the substantial pressure on my bladder. *Note to self: Do not drink a whole bottle of green tea before going to sleep after a seventy-two hour shift.* Waking up from sleep has never been easy for me. Since I was a little girl, my mother and father always told me I could sleep through a concert, tornado, or a train wreck. Truth.

I was in the middle of the weirdest dream. My mother and father were there. I can't quite remember much else which isn't uncommon for me. Although from the sweat dripping off my face onto my pillow, it was not a good dream. *Oh no!*

Opening my eyes slowly, I turn my head to face my phone blaring loudly on the bedside table. I realize it's not the alarm, but a phone call is coming in. Glancing toward the window, I see it's still dark outside. What time is it?

Grabbing my phone, I notice it's four o'clock in the morning. *Fuck! I've only been asleep a few hours.* My phone goes off again and I see a New York City number displayed on the screen. It doesn't belong to anyone I know. I hope my mother's okay.

As I answer the call, trepidation fills my soul. Something is wrong. I can feel it deep down in the marrow of my bones. *My dream ...* I've always had a sixth sense. The first time it happened, I was six years old. My puppy Bruiser was playing in the front yard with me. All of a sudden, I was swamped with a terrible feeling of sadness. And for a six-year-old, it was a bit overwhelming. Then a few moments later, Bruiser ran out into the road and was hit by a car. It was a very traumatic experience. Later on, I realized it was a warning. Being a logical person, this didn't fit into my world. So I kept it to myself. I've never shared it with anyone until I met my roommate and best friend Candie.

Someone on the phone repeats, "Hello, is anyone there?", breaking my trance.

"Oh, my apologies. My brain is a bit foggy. I just got off a seventy-two hour shift at the hospital. Hello. Who is this?"

"Miss Wren Bishop?" asks the caller.

"Yes, that's me. Who is this?" I repeat in a groggy tone.

"This is Sergeant Ryan with the NYPD 26th precinct. You are listed as the only relative to contact for a Ms. Katrina Bishop. Is this your mother?"

For a moment I can't seem to catch my breath. This can't be happening again. *Please, don't let it happen again.* Closing my eyes, I count to ten backwards, then answer in a mildly panicked tone, "Yes, Katrina Bishop is my mother. Is everything alright? Is she okay? Is she d—?"

The sergeant interrupts my anxiety. "Calm down, Miss Bishop. Your mother is alive. She was found wandering the streets of Manhattan last night in her night clothes. She was screaming profanities loudly at passersby, but it appeared as if she was talking to someone who wasn't there. Even when we apprehended her into custody, she was looking right through us. Your mother didn't even notice what was happening until we arrived at the hospital. When she finally came to her senses, the first person she asked for was you, Miss Bishop."

"Oh, thank god." I sigh in relief that my mother is alive, grateful I will see her again.

"Miss Bishop?" Sergeant Ryan prods. "When can you be here? Your mother needs a custodian. Someone to help make rational decisions for her treatment."

The relief that washes over me is instantaneous, the tightness in my shoulders giving rest as I take another deep breath. She's okay. My mother is still with me.

"Yes, of course, Sergeant Ryan. I understand. I will be there in a few hours. I'll take the next train to New York. Thank you, sir. Thank you so much. I'll see you soon."

When I disconnect the call, I feel my bed dip beside me and Candie's arm wraps gently around my shoulder.

"It's all going to be alright, Wren. You'll see."

I lean into her warmth and take in deep breaths. No need to cry over spilled milk, so I talk myself out of it. Candie's comfort will aid my aching heart until I see my mother in person.

The rest of the morning passes in a blur while

Candie packs me an overnight bag and walks me to the train station. I settle into my seat at the back of the half-empty train car, lean my head against the window, and close my eyes for a little while, drifting off into blackness.

I rouse from my nap when I hear the conductor announce over the speakers that we have arrived at Penn Station. After exiting onto the platform, I enter the bustling streets with my overnight suitcase pulling behind me. I capture the sights of people scurrying by, taxicabs racing to and fro, Jumbotrons lit with advertisements, and skyscrapers all decorating the street. I'm home.

I hail a taxi and begin my journey uptown to Mount Sinai St. Luke's Hospital where my mother is waiting. As we travel north in the bumper-to-bumper traffic, I take in the magical, familiar sights of the city. We pass Times Square, full of bright lights, shopping, and shows. Navigating at a slower pace, Central Park comes into view, a forest of green stuck right in the center of urban concrete. Truly beautiful. Next we come by the majestic Cathedral Church of St. John the Divine, its medieval Gothic pillars standing frozen in time and watching over all who enter.

A short time later, we arrive at Mount Sinai

Hospital. I exit the taxi and pull out the money to pay the cabby. Pulling my suitcase along the sidewalk, I enter the hospital. After checking in with the information clerk, I begin my long trek to the psychiatric wing of the hospital. I'm not shocked to find that my mother has been placed under around-the-clock watch. She's on the verge of a mental breakdown. Since the day I got mother's call my senior year of high school, she has never been the same.

*Tonight, we're going to party! It's my senior graduation night. A bunch of my classmates and I have big plans. Our parents booked a special event in Central Park for our graduating class. It's going to be epic.*

*Finishing up my makeup, I run my fingers through my long auburn locks. Looking in the mirror, I notice a young woman staring back at me smiling because all of my hopes and dreams are about to come true. In the fall I will be attending Harvard University's Pre Med program. I've wanted to be a doctor, like, forever ... just like my daddy. He's a highly respected cardiologist, one of the top in his field.*

*I button up my top, leaving the last several*

*open to reveal some cleavage, because when you got it, flaunt it, right?*

*My phone starts ringing, echoing off the walls of my room. It's my mother's ringtone,* Hot Mama *by Trace Adkins. Crazy, I know. What started out as a joke between me and my mother turned into her song. I've called her hot mama for years and when that song came out ... well, you know the rest.*

*Reaching over to the dresser, I clutch my phone and open it up, answering, "Hello, Hot Mama!"*

*"Wren..." Sniff, sniff. "Wren baby girl, I need you." My mother's heartfelt plea leaves me speechless.*

*"Wren, it's your father. There was a crash. Blood. Life flight. Hospital. Sending a car." I only heard parts and pieces. My brain began to shut down. No, no, no, no, NO! Not my daddy.*

Beep, beep, beep, beep. The sounds of a heart monitor machine serenade my ears. Somehow while walking down nightmare lane, I found my mother's room. A grey-headed, tall man in a white coat enters carrying my mother's chart. He gazes in my direction with an affectionate, reassuring smile.

"Good morning. Miss Bishop, I presume?"

"Yes, I'm Wren Bishop, Katrina's only daughter. Dr..."

"Dr. Kavanaugh. Do you know why your mother is here, Wren, if I may ask?"

I nod in recognition of his comment. "Certainly, doctor. I understand very well. My mother has been living in a realm of torture of her own making since my father died. Over the years, she has suffered from hallucinations, loosening of associations and psychosis. We've tried an array of medications and nothing has helped."

"I see you know what you're talking about. My apologies if I seemed harsh. Most families don't understand the severity of the disease your mother is suffering from." Dr. Kavanaugh nods.

"Thank you. I'm in my final year of residency at Mass General. I sought out help for her and you came highly recommended. The last time I spoke with my mother about a month ago, we discussed her appointment that was scheduled with you for last week. I'm assuming that's why you're here. Unfortunately I've just come off of seventy-two-hour shift rotations for two weeks. I'm totally exhausted and I haven't checked up on her."

"I see. Wren, your mother is going to need

twenty-four-hour observation for a short period. I understand that she isn't violent to herself or anyone else, but it doesn't mean it can't happen. I want to admit her into my program. It's intensive therapy and, of course, an arrangement of medications will be involved so that we can find the right fit for her. My goal is to make her better, help her live out the rest of her life in this reality and not the one she has conjured on her own."

Dr. Kavanaugh finishes up explaining all the details of his psychotic disorder diagnosis for my mother. He also explains that it will be my decision because I am her only living relative. The burden falls on me.

Later, I sit quietly by the window watching the birds fly through the evening sky while mother still sleeps. Dr. Kavanaugh said she had been sedated when she couldn't speak to me immediately and she should be waking up any time.

"Wren." A whisper. "Wren?"

I turn in time to see my mother disoriented and pulling at the cuffs on her hands. I hurry to her side to help ease her discomfort.

"Mother, it's me. I've come to take care of you."

"Oh, my little Wren. I knew you would come." A ghost of a smile captures her beautiful face.

And then everything goes to shit. Mother's face morphs into trepidation as she looks over my shoulder staring as if someone is standing behind me. I glance back, but no one is there.

"What's wrong, mother? Do you see him? Is he here?" I ask, because we've had this conversation time and time again since my father died. At first, it was painful to hear. Then, as time moved on and mother got worse, the tightness that came with thinking of my daddy lessened.

"I told you to leave me alone! Not here, not with our baby girl." Her yelling turns to tormented screeches and the nurses run into the room with a sedative, administering the drug as my mother continues to wail and cry.

I'm left feeling helpless. I love my mother so much and I hate to see her deteriorating one piece at a time. We were a happy family until that fateful night of my father's car accident.

Is it possible to love someone so much that even when one passes on, a part of them stays with the other? A soul mate? Even in death, you are forever linked?

My parents loved each other beyond words. It was obvious for anyone who knew them. They had found true love in each other. *Ugh!* I shiver at the thought. If this is what true love does to a person, count me out. I will never subject myself to the possibility of going crazy. I can never be like my mother.

# CHAPTER 3

**New York City, Present day**

*Aldin*

Slinking into the obscurity of blackness and shadows of the musty alley, I lie in wait. Tonight I will catch a glimpse of my family. Well, not my immediate family exactly, but three generations removed. Family, nonetheless.

My mission has been to see to my family's care since that night over two hundred years ago. Sure, I received my three wishes as Marcus had promised, but it came with a cost. So here I am, lurking in the darkness and catching peeks of my sister's offspring, making sure that they are well taken care of.

True to his word, Marcus set up my family with an abundant trust fund which has carried through the decades. I myself have access to all the money that I could ever want or need. The women are abundant, at my beck and call. And of course, the one thing I thought could never happen: immortality.

That's right, I am an Enchanted Immortal Vampire, a night dweller. Not the scary things that human nightmares are made of. We are the guardians of the night, and humanity's peacekeepers. The memories of when I first woke up are insignificant now. Although, I was anxious, yet at peace ... if that's even possible. A strange feeling settled over me, as if I was coming home...

*My eyes are heavy and I can't seem to open them. There is a pounding ache that fills my entire form. My body feels as if shards of glass are pressing into my skin, as if all the glass windows at the cathedral burst and I was their target. My stomach is rolling around and around, growling for something I've never felt. An urge not for food, but something else. I don't understand.*

*I hear a noise off to my right—footsteps that sound so loud, like they're walking all over my face. I press a hand to my head in hopes of relief. A door opens loudly and the footsteps descend* upon me. I growl low in my throat, an instinctive reaction, unsure if it's friend or foe who approaches.

Then I remember my last moments ... Oh my god! The fangs, the eyes. I jerk upright as my fatigued eyes dart around the room in the blinding light and landing on the last man I saw before blackness took me.

Leaning against a bedpost in a nonchalant manner is Lord Marcus Dalca. His piercing gaze is directed at me, a smile playing across his stoic face. Willing my eyes to focus, I observe him in the well-lit room and notice his eyes are a grayish black now with a red ring circling around the pupils and irises. He has an aristocratic air about him and his features are hard with high cheekbones, an elongated face, and firm lips that seems amused. He's beautiful for a man, a celestial-like quality to his aurora.

Taking a moment to catch my breath, I take in the lavish furnishings of my surroundings. In my current position, I'm on a majestic red mahogany oak four-poster bed with bedding to match the extravagant decor. Colors of deep garnet, golds, and emerald greens encompass the design. Carpets are placed carefully around the *hardwood floor in a stately way. Affluence oozes from everywhere.*

*What is this place? My throat is parched for a drink. Trying to muster any voice with which to speak, I finally croak out, "Where am I? What did you do to me? What are you?"*

*Wait, is that my voice? It sounds deeper— huskier, even—through my cracked throat.*

*With a soft laugh in his deep, strong voice, he shakes his head. "So many questions, my new apprentice. All in due time. First things first, though. You must feed," Marcus replies in his aloof tone.*

*"What does that mean??" I screech, fearful of the answer to come.*

*"Now, now, Aldin. All is well. You are getting everything you asked for and more." Marcus smiles broadly in a fatherly fashion. "I'm going to take care of you. But first, you need to feed. Drink from me."*

*Without delaying any further, he approaches and I watch in petrified fascination as his canines descend upon his wrist, slicing it up his forearm. My nostrils flare immediately, taking in the sweet aroma of the blood he is offering. Feeling the stick of my teeth against my bottom lip. My stomach rolls in anticipation or disgust, I can't be sure. I still don't understand what is happening to me, but instincts overrule logic as he presses his arm to my mouth. A luscious flavor of coppery goodness bursts across my tongue as I grab hold of his arm and take my first drink as an Enchanted Immortal.*

Shaking off the old thoughts, I see a car pull up outside the brownstone. A man exits the driver's side, heading around to the passenger. I watch patiently as he carefully helps the woman, round with child, out of the car. The couple walks up the steps and enters the dwelling.

I sigh to myself. The baby hasn't come yet, but she looks close. I'll need to keep a closer watch now, double my surveillance.

In my long life of immortality, I've been protecting my baby sister's descendants, making sure that if the need arises, I'm there to fulfill it— even without their knowledge of my existence. Over time, I've even slipped into a hospital or two in order to give my healing blood to a relative that would die otherwise, making full recoveries and living long and healthy lives, all the while baffling the doctors. This is my way of helping them.

Walking away and heading down the street, my thoughts are brimming with my family and my own lack of intimacy. How I wish I could have a family of my own.

"Bollocks! Not going there." I snap back to reality.

Running my hands through my wavy black hair and tugging roughly on the ends, the memory from my human years of a slight stick of pain eases my soul. No more wishes for me. I've had my fair share of my genie in the bottle.

Climbing onto my bike, I breathe in the fresh crisp air of fall.

"It's a nice night for a ride," I say to myself.

Cranking up the Harley, I feel the power of the 1820cc engine between my thighs as I pull out of the dark parking lot. I cruise through the streets, dodging cars and pedestrians until I've made it to the outskirts of town. Pulling the throttle back, I lean into the wind feeling alive again.

I ride through the New York countryside. Enjoying the solidarity of nothing but the rumble of my engine and my thoughts go blank while taking in the beauty of the night. For a brief time, I leave everything behind and just enjoy the harmony of the darkness.

# CHAPTER  4

## *Aldin*

As I navigate back to the city, the discussion with Marcus earlier today hounds me. There are a few locals south of the city who have gone missing. It seems suspicious and could be a human killing, but Marcus wants it checked out. The missing humans vary in age, sex and race. There is no pattern to it. "Something's off with the whole situation," I mumble into the wind. Too many inconsistencies that lead him to believe it could be supernatural, an Enchanted Immortal Vampire, Shifter, or Necromancer. It's not settling with me, either. Therefore, I will obey.

Marcus' enrichment of my life as an Enchanted Immortal began the day I awoke as a vampire, and he has continued teaching me over the centuries.

When he first created me, he sheltered me, kept me under his wing and out of harm's way. I strived to learn everything I could. I was a sponge, soaking in a life I never knew existed outside of my humble beginnings. He made sure I had the best tutors money could buy, to teach me how to speak, how to act, and about business. He set a high standard for me, and I excelled under his guidance and leadership. I learned about survival and different martial arts techniques as well.

He insured that I was educated in history, art, and every beautiful thing the world could offer. "I'm prepping you for great things," he would say. But, I knew he was grooming me to one day step into his shoes and rule the Enchanted Immortals in his stead. I became his number-two man after ten years of studying hard in order to one day take over all his vast wealth and kingdom. I'm fluent in many languages and run the board for Dalca Worldwide Services, Inc., among many other businesses for him. He submerged me into a culture that was alluring, exotic ... and is now my life.

Marcus is an Immortal. He told me his family hailed from Egypt, a place I've visited once with him after my transformation, and many times since the age of airplanes. He is a naturally-born

Immortal, centuries old. He's never told me his exact age, and out of respect for him, I've never asked. He shares what I need to know, and for me, that has been enough. His mother, father, and brother were lost in a battle which happened eight centuries ago. Truly hard to believe Marcus is so old when he looks to be no older than thirty. It's no surprise that his wealth is extensive and that he also presides over all Enchanted Immortals as the King. He is one of three original Immortals living today. Many seek his guidance and wisdom.

But even with all his success and importance, Marcus is lonely. I believe it is one of the reasons he found and turned me. I've been like a son to him and he, a father to me. Unlike the Enchanted Immortal Shifters and Necromancers, procreating as a vampire has never occurred. We cannot have children in the biblical sense; Marcus' line was the exception.

I am the only human he has shared his blood with to become an Enchanted Immortal since he lost his parents. Marcus assumed the role of father as well as maker when I began my immortal life, taking the place of my deceased father. Actually, over the years, he has treated me much better than my own father ever did. I know that he wants to step down and let me assume his lineage. "Lead from the sidelines" is how he puts it. I'm just not sure I'll ever be the man he tries to groom, yet I will always try to succeed for him.

During some of our long talks, he has told me of a female from the past with yearning laced in his voice. Through stories of her, and his own desire to find one, he conveyed upon me the miracle of finding a true mate. I've come to realize, it is a widely known fact and sought by many Enchanted Immortals, especially the ones that have been around a long length of time.

Despite the fact that Marcus has said many times he will never have a true mate, he had strong feelings for a human female. She had tempted him like no other, making his blood boil in all the right places. But then she vanished, disappeared one afternoon on her way home from the market without a trace. For a time, Marcus said he went a little crazy trying to find her. They weren't bonded and he had no way to locate her.

He believed she passed on to the afterlife. Even though he never saw her body, it was for the best. He often felt she was better off because a relationship between a human and Immortal was doomed from the start with all the differences between them.

I wonder if she was his true mate. Maybe his strong feelings weren't random because he has never spoken of another like her. I know Marcus longs for a mate, someone to complete him in every way. Maybe one day, his desires will come to fruition. Until then, my company will have to do.

I have been in the presence of several true mate couples over my time as an Enchanted Immortal. Bonded pairs who profess this one true and miraculous phenomenon. The union is apparent, undeniable. Anyone can see the way they drift together as sure as waves crashing to the shore.

Normally a true mate bond occurs between someone within the Enchanted Immortal race. True mates between humans and Enchanted Immortals are rare, but not unheard of. I can count them on one hand.

It's been explained that when you taste the blood of your true mate, your other half is found, and your souls forge into one. A connection immediately transpires which grows and forms into a life altering need for each other ... or so I've been told.

But again, it's not my reality. Personally, not

my forte. I prefer to dominate with no strings attached. I'm not looking for something that will never happen. If Marcus hasn't found his mate and he's centuries old, what are the chances of me finding mine? I will never again wish for things that are not within my reach.

Don't get me wrong. I appreciate the kindness Marcus showed me the last two hundred years. Although the simple fact is, I'm an Enchanted Immortal Vampire, a night dweller with no chance of having a real family like the Necromancers and Shifters.

At times, I have pondered why we were created. Yes, we are keepers of Earth and help with the balance for humans. Enhanced Immortal Vampires watch over the night. During my time, I've had to kill supernaturals and humans. I've always been able to escape and conquer my foe, except on one occasion. I'll never forget it. I was attacked by four rogue vampires shortly after being created while I was still considered a fledgling. The prospect of my immortality coming to an end when it had only just began ... that was something I couldn't fathom. Out of nowhere, Marcus appeared and rescued me, our innate connection bonding us. I realize that our relationship is more than master and servant; we share a bond intertwined by blood. And, for the next century, I never left his side.

Yet, thinking of where I was before and where I am now, I will not complain. I'm grateful, even though I missed my mother and Ana terribly. That was the hardest part of my turning. They had to believe I was dead. Again, my reality. I watched over them from the shadows. Ana married a wealthy shipmaker and had six children, three boys and three girls. Mother lived many happy years watching each grandchild grow. At their deaths, I took on the responsibility of caring for our lineage. It grew harder and harder as the children-turned-adults died—no one left to remember me.

Dipping into the curve of the road as low as my bike will allow without crashing, I speed through the night. Pushing the boundaries, always living on the edge, is my constitution. I can't be killed in the normal human fashion, so I ride hard, live harder, and play the hardest. Always at the extreme.

Getting back to the city, I find my home, Dalca Towers, and roar into the parking garage. I psych myself up for a night of debauchery. Parking my bike, I proceed to the elevators as I peel off the layers of body armor.

I nod to the doorman as he opens the elevator

for me. "Thanks, Mike. How are you this evening?"

"Good sir. An excellent night for a ride," Mike confirms.

"Yes, it is." I nod with a smile and wait silently beside him as we ride to the top floor.

Mike's been with us now for about fifty years and doesn't look a day over twenty-five. I study him as we ride the elevator up to the penthouse. Like the rest of us, Mike is built like a linebacker or a tree trunk, some might say. Ripped muscles hard as stone with keen senses: smell, sight, hearing, strength, and speed. Our bodies change once created not just on the inside, but the outside.

We're virtually indestructible. The only way an Enchanted Immortal can be killed is a stake to the heart in order to stop the blood flow, followed by decapitation, then burning the body to ashes.

When I first looked at myself in the mirror after I woke up, the man staring back at me had similarities, but vast differences. I gained almost six inches in height, which put me close to the seven-foot range. The already-defined muscles I had from working at the shipyard became even more prominent, more powerful. My body was huge all over—not exactly in the bodybuilder way, but close enough. It was amazing how different I was everywhere. No longer a boy, now a man ... no, not a man: an Enchanted Immortal Vampire.

Thanks to urban mythology and new age literature out in the world, people today perceive Enchanted Immortals as horrible, menacing beings, glamorizing only bits and pieces. So far from the truth. Then again, the glittery, sparkling vampires which started as a book series and became a box office hit are somewhat correct.

As an Enchanted Immortal Vampire, we can go out during the day, but we don't sparkle. However, most choose not to because of the caustic burns that plague us if we do. Not a pretty thing to see or get rid of. Our bodies will heal; it just hurts like hell, and I'm not a fan of that kind of pain. Still, it's not unheard of for a vampire to walk through Central Park during the daylight hours—under the cover of the canopy of trees, of course. One of the many companies we own developed a way for vampires to be in the sunlight without burning. Another invention Marcus' reign has benefited Enchanted Immortals. The protective gear that's been created for us helps us to acclimate and life is a little easier when going outside. I never leave home without it.

All Enchanted Immortals require blood to

survive. We do not kill our human donors. Again, that's an urban myth that, maybe at one time many centuries ago, was practiced. The drinking of another's essence is a very sensual act. The donors that we do find out in the human world draw great pleasure, heightened orgasms over and over during the feeding, and in the end are none the wiser. The saliva in our mouth has a healing property, so we leave no holes behind.

Another sensory embellishment is the power of suggestion over a human's mind. When we feed, we leave a positive memory of the whole encounter. The knowledge of what transpired is never remembered. Just one more way of ensuring we stay a secret.

At the same time, all Enchanted Immortals can share blood, however it's not the life-sustaining blood we need to exist; only human blood has that property. If an Enchanted Immortal decides to share his or her blood with a human, the recipient is given extended lifespan, is healed of diseases, and experiences more attuned senses. That's one more reason I share my blood when necessary with my kin.

In regards to the Vampire legend that we can't eat human food, we actually can and do, upon occasions that require it. Food, however, is tasteless to us, like the plastic fruit sold in stores. They look original and as tasty as the real thing, but pop it in your mouth and it's rubbery, chewy, and unsatisfying. I enjoy a good shot of whiskey from time to time. Again, it doesn't affect my taste buds, but the burn in my throat reminds me of being human.

We have blood banks we pay to provide blood when we can't get it fresh, which helps us survive in the shadows and not call any attention to our species. We also have a "spokesperson" to be the face of our corporation, someone in the ranks that can interact with humans for a little while because humans are so curious about everything. Then a few years later, another takes their place to make sure that no one suspects that we never age. Although we have had human partners, a select few have the knowledge of our existence—very few.

There are a handful of renegade supernaturals that were created and should never have been because their body rejected the gift. They plague the world by devouring their donors. They feel it is their right for being at the top of the food chain. And those are the ones that we take down. One of the first things I learned to do was hunt the others when one goes rogue.

Under Marcus' leadership, we practice the Enchanted Immortal lifestyle safely. It is a tight-knit community that thrives even though we do not partake in many of the human aspects of daily life. The Necromancers and Shifters have the ability to create life similar to humans, so they blend into the human world easily. Necromancers are gifted with magical powers, and Shifters can fluidly take the shape of anything breathing.

As the glass elevator doors slide open, the music blares loudly throughout the open penthouse. My eyes roam to the bodies grinding together to and fro on the dance floor. The scents of blood and sex assault my senses. I'm wound up tight and in need of a release. Not the normal kind. It's been a long day, a long week, a long century, and my desire is to get lost in a warm, sexy body for the night.

Seeking out my prospect, I walk slowly towards my bounty. Sitting on the lap of another is the woman I want for tonight: Nubia. I reach down and grasp Nubia's dark hair at the base of her neck while picking her up off of the man she is currently fucking with her lips.

Leaning down close to her ear, I whisper, "Be

in my room in fifteen minutes." I release her and head for the bar to score my first of many whiskey shots of the night. No need to worry about Nubia. I know she'll comply; they always do.

# CHAPTER 5

*Aldin*

I sense her presence in my room before opening the door. *Good pet.*

Nubia originates from Egypt. Her body is long and lively with full supple breasts and an olive-toned skin that drives any man crazy. Her hair falls long down her back like sheets of black silk. She has oval, dark eyes and lush, red lips that can suck a cock like no tomorrow. She is a Mediterranean beauty, an Enchanted Immortal Shifter.

Enchanted Immortal Shifters have the ability to take the form of any breathing, organic life form—their gift from the gods. They still require blood and, unlike vampires, they can breed.

Instead of coming through my chamber doors, I go to the secret doorway which leads through my closet. My closet reminds me of my flat from long ago. It's the same size, anyway. I change quickly into just a pair of sweats and grab the implements I'll use for the night and walk into my room.

Nubia is kneeling naked by the bed, eyes down, palms on her thighs—exactly how I instructed her when we began so many years ago. We have been roleplaying the last seven decades and my sexual hunger beats alongside survival feeding that I require to live. Feeding is an erotic experience between a donor and host. A symbiotic relationship is formed and sexual gratification is induced by the piercing of the skin when thousands of endorphins are released into the bloodstream of the donor, instantly causing orgasmic pleasure.

Over the years, the stimulation I required for sexual release has escalated to dominating a willing submissive, pushing my partner beyond the normal boundaries set by the mind and allowing the senses to direct the flow of pleasure. Control is key. Self-discipline is tested. The act of restraining someone at their will and having total power while the hunger and desire builds never changes. I thrive in these moments because I feel human once again.

Tonight we will travel back to the 1800s. "Your

master requires blood, wench. Are you willing to feed his hunger?"

"Yes, master," she responds immediately.

I circle her and decide what device I want to use. Lacing my fingers through a black leash, I approach her. She remains still and doesn't move. I bend down and clasp the collar around her neck and lead her to the horse in the corner of the room.

"Straddle," I order as she complies, bending her knees and laying forward with her arms spread wide. I fasten the cuffs over her wrists, binding her knowing that she could break free if she wanted, but she chooses to submit to my will. My cock twitches, relishing in the small victory. It's all about control.

I return to the table and place the leash back in its place and grab the next item of choice: my riding crop. I thumb the end as I contemplate how long I will torture her with pleasure.

"You will not release until I grant permission."

"Yes, master."

"Only I allow you pleasure while you are in this room."

I weave the crop softly over her back, drawing figure eights in the air, knowing her sense of hearing can determine exactly where it is. Time slowly passes as I continue, waiting for the right moment to strike. I'm allowing the unknown time to build her anticipation.

Using my quick reflex, I pop the inside of her thigh close to her already weeping pussy. A slight moan escapes her lips. She's enjoying this foreplay. I've learned over our encounters that Nubia's sexual pleasure borders the line of pain. The more intense sensual torture inflicted, the more pleasure she receives. We both are searching for the human fix.

The crop softly follows the long lines of her arms inward towards her breast. Her breathing has grown shallow and quick. She's fighting the urge to move and she knows I will end everything if she does. After years of engaging in our sexual acts, I recognize her weaknesses and enjoy the rush of triumph as the crop meets her fleshy breast and we begin the tit-for-tat again.

This time, the crop is tracing the inside of her heel, softly touching. I retract the crop and a loud echo is heard when it connects with the wood floor below. My hands move towards her tanned ass and I massage the smooth flesh. She reacts by arching into my palms. I lightly squeeze and release, then trace the crease of her ass with my thumb to her forbidden entrance.

A hard knock on the door disturbs my exploration. I walk casually to the door, even as rage burns into my body for being interrupted.

"What?" I harshly call through the door. No need to open it; the Enchanted Immortal on the other side can hear me clearly.

Nick, my right-hand man, responds, "You're needed at the hospital, sir."

Instantly, my mood morphs into happiness; helping my family is ultimately what I exist for now. My nightly playtime is of no consequence anymore, and time is cut short with Nubia in order for me to get to the hospital for the arrival of the next baby in the family. *Just in case*, I tell myself. At this point, the baby is coming early. My blood may be needed and I'm willing to give it.

As I leave Nubia bound in my room, I reflect on all the women in my life. Nubia indulges my sexual deviance, plays games, and takes whatever I desire because it suits her, even though she's part of our dominant species. Not that Nubia isn't satisfied, because I give *all* my women satisfaction, but all they will ever be to me is a great fuck, my playthings, one of many that appease my hefty appetite. There are no feelings or emotions tied to any of these women. I don't cuddle, do the "lovey dovey" thing. Just not my style. I've accepted my role in this world. I'm a dominant species with a wicked appetite. Such is my life, and for now, it is all I crave or desire.

# CHAPTER

**6**

*Wren*

Waking up to the sun shining brightly in my face is not my idea of a good wake-up call. I throw my hands across my eyes, blocking the penetrating sun coming in through the floor-length windows in my bedroom. My head is a foggy mess from yesterday's long hours at the hospital. My brain is trying to tell me it's time to wake up again, but my body is totally and completely exhausted by the clusterfuck that was the day before. There were four new babies born and my time was spent running around taking care of the new lives.

As the fog lifts from my brain, one newborn in particular has shipwrecked in my head. A preemie. There were a few complications at first, but I was able to stabilize the baby and before I left last night, she was breathing on her own—still in an incubator, but stable. Also, I'm unsure of what I saw. I think my overworked brain played tricks on my eyes. There was a man lurking in the corner of the room with me in the prenatal intensive care unit. I felt his presence … and then it was gone. That's crazy, right?

I'm a spiritual person. I believe in the supernatural and want to believe we aren't the only beings lucky enough to be alive in the universe. Having a sixth sense of my own—a warning bell—it helps me believe. But that was just plain weird. Whatever it was, I felt a sense of peace from it, yet I could also feel its power. Apparently I was the only one to feel the strange presence, so I let it go.

It was a cray-cray kind of day. Being a pediatric doctor, it's not uncommon. That's what makes me, Dr. Wren Bishop, tick.

Gracelessly removing my limbs one by one from the comfort of my sheets, I roll up and out of bed. Time to get ready for another day at the hospital. I stumble through the apartment to the kitchen.

"I need coffee," I mumble.

I shuffle blindly over to the coffee pot and pour myself a piping hot cup of the life-giving brew.

After I've added my cream and sugar, I walk carefully to the bar and sit down on one of the stools.

Standing in the kitchen making breakfast is my roommate, Candie. "Good morning, sleepyhead." Her voice bellows throughout our coveted classic six apartment and I squint my eyes at her.

"Who says it's good?" I ask her, but I know what's coming next.

"Oh, Wren. The sun is shining and we've been given another day," she answers. "What more could you ask for?"

Give her lemons and she'll just make lemonade.

Candie prepares two plates and carries them over to the bar for us to eat. That's how she rolls. Every morning without fail, she makes breakfast. And let me tell you, it's a welcome treat because I do not like to cook. It's not that I can't; I just don't like to.

As I dig into the delicious vegetable omelet Candie created this morning, I keep my thoughts to myself. I love my life, really. I have a thriving practice and I'm constantly being consulted on high profile cases for children. I'm totally busy day and night, but sometimes my life is lonely. On the outside, it appears I have everything because I have my work with its challenges and my best friend Candie. Still, every so often when I see parents like the ones of the preemie baby girl last night, I long for ... well, something that I know I'll never have. Not just an all-consuming love like my parents shared, but children. It's just not in the cards for me. My work is my life. I clamp down on Pandora's box quickly and turn to face Candie.

"This is so yummy, Candie. You really outdid yourself today."

She beams brightly back at me and I feel that I'm okay for a little while. I can forge ahead.

"Thanks. Hey what time do you get off work today? There's this really cool band playing at the club tonight and I'd love for you to come down and we could spend some quality BFF time." Candie unloads her prospects for tonight.

"I think I may be able to cut out a little bit early, since yesterday was so fucking crazy. But it all depends on whether or not any of my new patients arrive today or not. You never know." I add the last part because we've tried a night out before and I had two new babies arrive instead.

"Cool! I'll text you the times. Hopefully all will go well." Candie smiles again as she stands to take her plate to the sink. "Besides, there are some really hot men coming in with this band. You could totally go for a one-night stand, Wren. It's been too long!"

Cringing at her comment because she's so right, I head over to the sink with my plate to rinse off before putting in the dishwasher.

"Oh I know, I've been going through batteries a lot more over the past few months." We both giggle at my banter. "I could really go for a tall drink of water!"

I leave Candie to go get ready for a fun-filled day of babies. I start to hum a tune and dance like I'm insane. Well, maybe I am a little. Life's too short for wishing and hoping for things to happen. I should know. We have to make the best of what we have.

"Whoa! Where the hell did that come from?" I scold myself. Candie must be rubbing off on me.

We've lived together here in Manhattan for the past five years since I graduated medical school. We met as college freshmen and have been inseparable ever since. Candie has shared some of my darkest moments, like my mother's meltdown and admittance into the psychiatric facility. Even though our careers are vastly different, we click.

Continuing down the hall to my room and the shower that awaits, I hum the rest of the way. Maybe today will be different. Maybe tonight, I'll meet the man of my dreams. *Yeah, right.* Not going to happen. Nope.

Though, some one-on-one action is what I need.

As the waterfall shower sprays down on and around my parched body, I consider all that transpired last night. Brief snippets of a massive figure with jet black, wavy hair flows through my conscience. He's silent yet intrusive. Erotic and baffling. I only caught a brief glimpse of the shadowy figure, and then when the baby took a turn for the worse, everything changed. It didn't make sense. In all reality, that baby should not be alive, but a miracle happened within the few brief moments I felt *his* presence. An angel from heaven? Why did I see him and no one else did?

It reminds me of an encounter when I was a freshman in college. I was walking home one night from the library and was jumped by two burly guys in the alley between the dorms. I screamed, but no one was around to hear me. Then out of nowhere, a dark figure rose from the shadows. He carried with him a power in the air, thick and obtrusive.

From the corner of my vision, I watched as the lone figure yanked one of the men assaulting me and tossed him through the air into the adjacent wall as if he weighed nothing. The pressure from the second attacker eased as my eyes popped wide open.

My brain couldn't fathom what it was witnessing. The dark hero briefly looked at me and said, "Run," as he leaned over one of the assailants. That was all the push I needed to scramble to my feet and hightail it outta there. I never spoke of what happened that night, and I never again walked home alone either. There were no reports of an attack on the news or radio. If it weren't for the bruises on my arms from the attack, I would've thought it was all a horrible nightmare or I was going insane.

My mother's suffering reminds me that I can't think that way. That's how mother ended up with a one-way ticket to the loony farm. I'm not going there.

I push away the thoughts. I'm obviously super tired. It was my expertise that brought that child through the critical circumstance, right? It's the only logical explanation. Even *I'm* having a hard time believing it.

After washing my hair along with my cracks and crevices, I exit the shower and get ready for work.

# CHAPTER 7

*Wren*

Arriving at the hospital a little earlier than I'd planned, I have just enough time to stop at the Starbucks and grab a coffee: a mocha latte with whipped cream and a dash of cinnamon with a double shot. Just the way I like it. *Mmmmm.* Inhaling the chocolatey goodness, I enter the hospital and head up to the prenatal ICU.

I check in first with my preemie baby girl patient. "Lana" is posted on the card attached to her crib. Her parents named her overnight. She's bundled up tight in her blankets, a shock of dark wavy hair showing. Instantly my thoughts lead back to the dark presence I encountered last night. Lana's breathing is stable and she seems to have thrived overnight. It's a miracle.

I notice her parents in the corner of the room huddled together with such tenderness and love. I move closer to speak to them. "Good morning, Mr. and Mrs. McCaffrey. It seems you have a fighter."

Even just above a whisper, my voice carries through the small room along with buzzes and blips of the monitors contained in the unit.

"Lana ... I really like that name, by the way," I go on. "She seems to be doing really well this morning. Her vitals are stable and she's breathing rather well for a preemie. After the touch-and-go last night, I'm impressed." I give them much deserved hope. "I'd like to do a few more tests just to make sure everything is functioning properly inside of her. I'll need consent, of course, but it's just routine. Like I said, she seems perfect. A miracle." I finish up with my observation of how Lana is progressing.

Her parents seem bewildered yet hopeful. In awe and grateful, Mr. and Mrs. McCaffrey seem pleased with the good news. I'm happy to give it. After obtaining their agreement, I let them know I'll be back later or tomorrow with the results, although some may take a few days longer. I leave the couple and go to the nurse's station. I order the necessary tests and move along to my next patient.

I continue checking on all the babies born the day before while making my rounds to visit with parents and their new bundles of joy. No new arrivals today. So far so good.

Around lunchtime, I head to the break room for a bit of R&R, at least until I'm needed in an hour or so. I pop some lunch in the microwave, then eat the spongy-tasting cooked dinner as if it's a gourmet meal. Well, I'm trying to. *Ugh!* Chicken enchiladas from the freezer.

Afterwards, I find one of the semi-soft cots in the on-call area adjacent to the break room. I'm trying to relax from the hectic morning. Before shutting down and drifting off to sleep, I set my phone alarm to wake me up in an hour. A power nap will be awesome!

I jerk awake suddenly with an awareness of being watched. The same ominous feelings from the ICU last night seizes me. Scanning the room with only my eyes, I see a figure from the corner of my vision. I jolt upright as I feel big warm arms wrap around my body. Struggling to get loose, I can't see anything from the wide chest my face is thrust into. Panic floods my senses, followed by a sudden sense of peace. *What the—?* I calm from the warmth. My nostrils are filled with a welcome scent of masculinity, woodsy fresh and man. I close my eyes again, reveling in the sensations that are rolling through my system while a heavy hand slowly, seductively strokes my hair. I enjoy the whisper-soft presence of his voice as he holds me and quiets my fears. Before long, I succumb to the ministrations, drifting back to sleep, dreaming of a faceless mysterious man that haunts me.

## *Aldin*

Stroking her hair softly and whispering comforting words is not something I'm used to. Not my norm. But I can't help the feelings that are overwhelmingly clear in my mind. This woman belongs to me. I have an inherent, instinctual need to protect this fragile human woman in my arms. I can't explain it, but I must.

After seeing the lovely doctor last night in the prenatal ICU room, I was immediately obsessed with her and knew something was different about her. She could sense me, even when I was cloaked. *Only mates can feel other mates.* I fled the hospital after aiding the newest member to the family. I went for another bike ride to try and clear my head. We haven't even officially met yet, but my thoughts were owned by the mysterious Dr. Bishop. An aligning of delicate tendrils pulls me to her. I had to see her again. On the ride over this morning, I confessed to myself it was just to check on my niece, Lana. Then I saw her again. All sensibility faded away and I yearned to touch her.

Unsure of how to approach, I just watched her, carefully cloaking myself as she finished up her lunch and then took a nap in the adjoining room. I watched her in fascination while she carefully rested her coat out on the chair beside the bed and set her phone alarm. I am baffled by how beautiful this creature is. *No, not creature—human.* Her chestnut hair was tied tightly on top of her head in a bun, a few wisps flowing down the sides of her beautiful, round face. She has an angelic face with high cheekbones and round blue eyes that compliment her overall attractiveness. She's tall for a human woman, maybe around five-ten. And the curves of her body scream out to me, calling to me. Dr. Bishop is perfectly made for me.

I feel her stir from my induced, hypnotic sleep and drop her gently back down onto the makeshift bed. I don't understand these feelings. Is this the mating? Have I found my true mate? Shaking my head and tucking her in, I leave Wren to her sleep.

As an Enchanted Immortal Vampire, I don't need to sleep, but humans do, and she was up late last night taking care of the newest addition to my family.

I walk away from the woman who now plagues me. I have to find out what all this means. Is it just an attraction like all the others? No. Everything is different with this woman. She calls to me like no other. Could she be my mate?

Heading down to the garage where Dr. Bishop's car and my bike are parked, I survey my surroundings. Business matters weigh heavily on my mind along with my newest interest... "Wren." Saying her name on my tongue fires a desire and longing within my soul.

After I carefully put on my protective gear, tightening down the flaps and zippers of my jacket and gloves, I throw my leg over the seat of my Harley. Cranking it up, I rev the engine as I pull out of my space. There are dealings that must be attended to for the moment. *In a little while, my Dr. Bishop.*

Later in the evening, I'm back at the hospital hiding in the shadows as I see Dr. Bishop walking towards her car. I suck in my breath from the sensual beauty she exudes. My dick stirs between my legs and I have to adjust myself. Not wearing her usual doctor attire, she's dressed in a skirt that trails just above her knees with a pair of delicious fuck-me boots trailing down her long legs. The halter top accentuates her ample breasts with a wrap thrown around her shoulders. Her hair is a bounty of russet curls trailing round her face, shoulders and back. My fangs ache as I long to claim her as mine.

"Bollocks," I whisper to myself. "What are you doing to me?" I'm caught in her snare.

She approaches her car and gets inside, none the wiser that she is in the midst of her greatest admirer. Starting up my bike, I wait for her to pull out so I can follow her. I long to talk to her, to get to know the woman. The longer I was away from her today, the more my mind solidified my need. I have found my true mate.

Dr. Bishop reverses from her parking spot and travels out onto the busy street. I follow closely behind, but not too close. After a few blocks she pulls into the parking garage of a popular night club—one we do business with. She exits her car and goes inside. Because I'm captivated by the attraction, I pursue with hopes of talking to my beautiful doctor. I'm smitten.

# CHAPTER 8

*Wren*

The music blasts through the speakers, caressing my body, and igniting a fire deep within. I'm still thinking about my nap at the hospital. Someone was in the room with me, treasuring me as if I was a precious jewel. A longing inspired from the encounter wraps around me, although it feels like something ... *other*. I'm not sure about the hows or the whys, but it's a feeling I just can't shake. My intuition is going haywire, warning me to be cautious.

Walking around the wall of people to the opposite end of the bar, I see Candie doing what she does best: talking. She's behind the bar flipping glass bottles and pouring drinks, all while smiling and chatting up the customers. She's awesome.

Candie received her business finance degree from Harvard. Now, she's co-owner of this amazing night club. I'm her silent partner. She's a hands-on type boss and won't ask anyone to do anything she wouldn't do herself, always sticking to bartending, which she loves the most.

She spies me after her latest bottle flip and walks over, leaning against the bar to give me a hug. "Hey, Wren. So glad you made it."

"Thanks, me too. I wasn't sure, but it all worked out. I let my hair down and I'm ready to have some fun! What's on tap?"

She nods with a warm smile. "Well, we have a couple of new things, but I think I know just what you'll like, sista. Be right back."

Candie walks off to make me a drink. I take a deep breath, scanning the room for prospects for the night. No one in particular catches my eye. Shrugging, I turn back around just as Candie walks toward me with a tall glass of beer in one hand and a shot of something dark in the other. Smiling brightly, she sets the beer in front of me.

"This is a new honey wheat specialty beer crafted locally. It has a sweet taste, you're gonna love it! And this," she adds, holding up the shot, "is top shelf whiskey and makes it a boilermaker." She pours the shot into the beer and peers across the bar at me with anticipation.

"Alrighty then. Bottoms up!" I say as I pull the sweating glass to my lips.

I take a big gulp and set the glass down gently on the bar. The combination of beer and whiskey burn down my throat while causing a warm feeling as it settles into my stomach. I instantly feel the alcohol taking root, relaxing my tense muscles. I wipe my mouth with the napkin Candie tossed my way as my lips turn up into a crooked smile.

"That's damn good, Candie. The beer by itself is smooth, delicious. Add the whiskey and it takes it to a whole new level."

"Yep, I knew you'd approve. Enjoy, BFF. I'll be back in a bit to check on you. I'm off in an hour and a half. Oh, and Wren? Try not to use the number rule when looking for a bed buddy." Candie saunters away as I sip on my new favorite drink.

Ha! She's crazy if she thinks I won't. I have this number rule, as Candie likes to call it. It's three strikes and you're out. Pretty simple. But at the same time, it's three yummies and you're in. It's my way of weeding out unwanted attention or potential stalkers. Hey, at least it works!

As I'm drinking the delicious boilermaker, I

survey the crowded bar again. It was loaded when I first walked in, but now it's bursting at the seams. I catch the eye of a tall dark and handsome figure leaning against the other end of the bar sipping on what looks like the same drink I have in my hands. He appreciates my stare by holding his glass up and nodding. I can't make out his eyes from this distance, but one corner of his mouth is turned up, anchoring me to his presence. Nodding back at him, he pushes off the bar and starts toward me.

The air sizzles and I gasp. I'm swamped by the same ominous feeling from the hospital. He's familiar, yet unknown. I shake it off, blaming it on the beer as I watch as the most mouthwatering hunk of a man strolls my way. At first glance, I'm struck by how enormous he is. At least six-and-a-half feet tall and full of raw, male power, he's a man that makes me feel short at my unusually-tall-for-a-woman height. Dark, unearthly eyes gaze intently toward me. Tight-fitting black jeans snuggle his muscular legs, pulled over biker boots and a black long-sleeved shirt stretched taut over an extensive chest. *Yummy #1.*

When he finally gets to me, he leans in and whispers in my ear, "Hello, Dr. Wren Bishop. I'm Aldin Kovac. Do you like the beer?"

*Wait, what? Stalker strike #1.* Apprehensively, I say, "Yes, it's delightful. But how do you know my name? Aldin, is it?" I study him skeptically.

"Your friendly bartender helped me out." He points with his head to Candie and her face confesses for her. She spilled the beans! *Note to self: talk to Candie about keeping me out of her extracurricular conversations.*

"Oh. Well, shit. Okay then. Are you having the same thing?" I clank my glass with his. His close proximity distracts me and causes lightheadedness from the power this man is wielding around me, over me, and pooling between my legs.

"Of course. After all, it comes from a distillery I own. It is exquisite." His black, piercing eyes are stalking me, laying claim on my body.

*Did he say he owns the delectable beer I'm drinking? Yummy #2!* My cheeks redden from the overheated excitement as I take in his majestic features. Aldin has the body of a god, ripped and panty-melting. His eyes are like the darkest midnight that scream hours of pleasure. His unblemished olive skin and hard face adds to the attractive man in front of me. Dark wavy curls surround his face, landing softly on his shoulders to give him a playboy vibe. Dangerous. Mysterious.

I'm instantly attracted to his brand of alpha. *Yummy #3—he's in.* Let's hope he agrees. And as if he can read my mind, Aldin caresses my cheek and then firmly grabs the back of my neck, pulling me in to him. The connection is instant. Our lips are a hair's breadth from each other. I lick my lips, anticipating what this dominant man will do next, and I'm ready for it.

He looks into my eyes and says, "Let's dance."

Left feeling breathless, I guzzle down the last of my drink and follow where he leads out onto the dance floor. Our bodies move sensually together, effortlessly, as if we were made for each other. This man can dance. He moves seductively to the beat of the music, stimulating and tantalizing, never taking his captivating, dark eyes off of me. Aldin pulls me to his front, grinding his massive erection against my ass while tightly gripping my hips. It's foreplay at its finest, claiming me, possessing me— his promise of things to come, if I accept it.

When the song *Thinking Out Loud* by Ed Sheeran comes on, Aldin pulls me closer, if that's even possible. Caressing my back in slow circles until his hands are cupping my ass, he stares down at my mouth while licking his sexy lips. The music takes us on a journey to another world, and time stands still. I'm held hostage by this big, beautiful man. Aldin moves in swiftly and seizes my mouth with his in a sensual, dominating assault. My brain explodes into a million blissful particles. Aldin continues to sway to the beat while rubbing his dick provocatively against my belly and the apex between my thighs, settling greedily there for the rest of the song.

We dance for one more song and then go back to the bar for another beer. I'm parched. My breathing is labored from the dancing and the foretaste of what Aldin is promising.

"Hey, you two," Candie sings as she sets down two more glasses of beer along with two waters in front of us.

"Thank you." Aldin's deep baritone voice washes over me, hot desire traveling down my belly.

"So I'm off in about fifteen minutes, Wren." Candie watches me in anticipation for the confirmation of my hook-up, which she had everything to do with. *Thank you very much.*

"I'm actually pretty tired, Candie. I think I'm gonna call it a night." I lean my head over and shrug, glancing at her with my eyes and a slight smirk to let her know my true meaning: *I'm taking*

*Aldin home with me.* My eyes dart slightly to Aldin, who stands so close our arms touch.

A smile too big for her face covers Candie's features. She gets my meaning. My drought is over. I chanced another look at the man I hope to consume tonight—*or let consume me*—and his eyes are hooded with a sliver of silver radiating out from the dark depths as he watches me closely. Candie backs up and walks away, giving me a double thumbs-up as she goes. I angle my body closer to this hunky man. I've gained a bit more liquid courage from the tasty beer, but hey, I know what I want.

"So, mister Aldin, maker of beer, sexy dancer and oh-so-delicious to the eyes. Would you like to go back to my place and continue this?" I push a finger into his rock hard pecs and then back to me.

Aldin stares at me, studying me like I'm a puzzle he has to figure out. His nostrils flare as if he's sniffing for something, and then his lips turn into a grin as he chuckles. He pulls my hand back and places soft, electrical kisses onto the back of my hand, then turns it over to pay the same attention to my palm and wrist. Darkened eyes monitor my response of his affection. My belly is playing flip-flop from his sultry attention.

"I thought you'd never ask, doc," he answers as he places a few large bills on the bar, never letting go of my hand.

He tugs me through the crowd, out the door, and into the dark night. Aldin's hand is firm on mine. A man on a mission. Strong and powerful. My insides start the happy dance as Aldin unlocks my car, gently placing me into the driver's seat. After my seatbelt is buckled tight, he captures my lips for another scorching kiss.

"My bike's right over there." He lingers in the door for a moment. "I'll follow you."

With one last kiss on the lips, he shuts my door and ambles toward a massive machine. I observe his strong legs as he straddles the bike. Aldin is gorgeous, with a capital G. *Maybe he'll take me for a ride*. Tonight, I'll get to ride *him*. Excitement coalesces over my sensitive skin. I pull out of the parking lot and we drive back to my place. The loud rumbling motor of Aldin's Harley penetrates my every thought as he follows behind me.

# CHAPTER 9

*Wren*

Stumbling through the door, limbs connected, we kiss passionately before and after I unlock the door to my apartment. Aldin is toting me into the apartment, gripping my ass in his much larger hands while my legs wrap around his hard torso. He carries me as if I'm weightless in his arms. *Mmmm, so strong.* I nibble, lightly biting the soft spot on his neck. I feel Aldin's cock pulse hard between my legs. Oh, he likes that. I continue my assault covering his neck, chin, and then move on to his lips.

Our tongues begin to duel, each fighting for dominance, but I soon relent as Aldin captures my tongue, sucking it into his hot mouth. Feeling his teeth clamp down softly, I figure he's letting me

72

know that he will be in control. Ecstasy flows hot and fierce through me, traveling down my spine and saturating my already dripping hot pussy. This is just what I need.

My body's desire amplifies while my head is confused with the emotional reaction of something akin to love. I've just met this man. How can I even think of love when I don't even know him?

Aldin the domineering alpha takes over as I feel my back against the door. His hard shaft is rocking my world, pushing in just the right places, caressing my clit with just enough friction that I begin to see stars. Aldin's foreplay becomes frantic as he rocks harder while passionately kissing me into oblivion.

"Aldin," I call out through my lust-filled haze.

His grip tightens as we bump into the couch. He stops and positions me on the floor in front of the couch, facing him.

"Strip. Now," he commands as he tosses his shirt behind me and kicks his boots off to the side.

I'm momentarily struck by the man standing in front of me, with his chiseled abs made for worshipping and a happy trail accented by wisps of dark hair on the well-formed V that vanishes below his jeans. I hold my breath as he pops the top

73

button. My anticipation of seeing where the trail will lead builds, and the idea of love creeps back and fills my heart with joy. *What the hell?* I don't believe in love at first sight like Candie does. I'm a scientist, and facts are facts. You can debate them all day long, but that won't change the outcome. Two plus two is four, right? The fact is, love takes time to develop and years to build into a relationship. Love doesn't happen at the snap of your fingers; lust does. *Hmph, wishful thinking. Glass-half-empty mentality.* Sometimes love doesn't happen at all. Hell, some people settle for companionship instead of living alone. Nothing more, nothing less.

My thoughts are interrupted by a low growl when he notices me standing in the same place he put me, still dressed.

"Wren, you have fifteen seconds to remove your clothing or I will be forced to rip them off of you."

The sound of his threat rings true, and instantly a part of me yearns to tempt him into carrying out his promise. *Again, what the holy hell?* Not knowing where this newfound hunger originated from, I stutter, "I... um..."

He breaks into my babbling, "Now, Wren."

His demand speaks to an unknown part of me, initiating actions of a rebellious nature. I slowly, methodically unbutton my top while holding his burning gaze, knowing I'm playing with fire. I want to burn. The last button unfolds and my blouse slides down my arms and lands on the couch. I reach for the zipper on my skirt and he's there gripping my hands behind my back with one of his, thrusting my chest eye-level.

"Naughty, little girl. Do you want me to spank your ass? That's what happens when you tempt the beast."

As I nod yes, his other hand rips my skirt down my body, and I'm standing before him in just my bra and thong. My heart is racing with excitement from his display of strength as he nuzzles my breasts and plants a long lick up the center. A growl escapes his throat and I'm panting, shaking, needing him to stop the pain building in my lower body. Then his teeth clasp my bra and his head jerks back as his bounty is revealed.

I watch as he leans back, marveling at his newfound treasure. His lust-filled gaze catches mine while he slowly lowers his lips for a taste. A moan escapes from me when his teeth clamp down on the tip of my nipple while his tongue laves at the same, his hand still holding mine behind my back—a display of power and dominance. The destroyed bra floats down my arms as I squirm trying to find release from the pleasure I am succumbing to when Aldin secures the fabric around my wrists, binding them together.

I mumble, startled from the pleasure drowning my senses when the silk from the tattered bra tightens. "Aldin ... What are you doing?" I ask, unsure of the bindings holding my arms in place.

A flash of red radiates in his lustful eyes as his hand covers my pussy, applying pressure on my clit. A smirk forms on his handsome face when he bends forward and caresses my nipple with his tongue. He takes his time before answering me.

"I'm allowing your fantasy to awaken, my lovely Wren. Fueling the fire burning within you for me. Fulfilling your dreams. Submit to me and let me feed your hunger," he commands, then his fingers slide between the fabric, rubbing my pleasure spot. "You're mine to possess. Mine to command. Mine to pleasure. You. Are. Mine."

The erotic jolts pulsing through my body at his words calm my mind as his sexual onslaught continues to drive me towards unimaginable pleasure. The upper part of my body leans into his arms, pleading for more, needing him to fulfill the ache churning within.

## *Aldin*

Wren's body surrenders at my words and her head falls back, accentuating her long, sexy neck. My gums ache as I yearn to sink my canines into her smooth, creamy skin while I feed from my true mate. Yes, Wren Bishop is mine. Everything I have ever wanted is standing before me on display, ripe for the taking. Mine. I want to shout it out loud. I no longer exist in this world. *I'm alive.* My shattered soul is mending with every moment we share.

I begin my assault on her once more, scraping my teeth along the life-giving blood vessel on the side of her throat. I fight the beast inside of me demanding I take what is mine. Her juices soak my palm as a finger penetrates her vagina. She's wet and tight as I try inserting a second one. Her moans grow louder and her body tightens as I finger-fuck her, setting a steady rhythm for her ultimate pleasure and massaging her clit with each thrust. She's on the edge as I strum her body like a well-played instrument. I stop, and instantly she is begging for more.

"Who's your master, Wren? Who owns this pussy?" My heart yearns to claim her as my mate, but the Vampire in me desires total domination.

She whimpers, "Please, I need..."

"Look at me, Wren," I order. "Who owns your body?"

She answers me with shuttered eyes. "You do, Aldin."

"Very good, my lovely Wren. Obey me and my pleasure is yours to take," I state and further explain her role in our first joining. "You are not allowed to come until I give you permission. Do you understand?" I want to savor our first time and learn what makes her tick.

She nods, acknowledging me, but I want her submission completely. My hand leaves her panties, snapping the flimsy material away. Lifting her, I sit down on the couch and place her over my lap. Her snowy white ass is lifted in the air, begging my hand to paint it blush as she squirms beneath my hold. My hand descends as a yelp fills the room, a faint handprint stamped on her skin—temporary ownership imprinted on my mate.

She moans; the little minx enjoys being dominated. She is my perfect match. Warmth surrounds me, knowing I am complete.

"You will answer 'yes, sir' when I question you, Wren," I tell her as my hand comes down once again.

"Yes, sir!" she cries out and her musky scent permeates the room.

I restate my command, asking for her submission. "You will not come until I allow it." Old habits die hard.

Sobbing from her arousal, Wren stammers, "Yes, sir."

"Good girl." The beast within purrs, sated by her answer.

I pat her reddened ass, sliding my fingers toward her puckered hole. She tenses for a moment, and then my fingers enter her dripping-wet pussy, slowly scissoring back and forth, in and out, again and again until her moans are consuming my every thought. Her body is tense as a ripple washes over her.

"Please, sir. I need to come," she pleads.

I release my hold around her waist and thrust my fingers deeper than before, pinching her clit at the same time.

"Come now for me, my lovely Wren."

Wren's body tenses as her moans escalate. A

chant gushes from her mouth. "Aldin, Aldin, Aldin." Her piercing cries soothe me to my core, releasing decades of turmoil and loneliness.

My final wish has come true. I've found my soulmate.

Knowing I'm the one that gave her unspeakable pleasure, I continue pumping, easing her back from the euphoria her body savored. My dick is throbbing, trapped in my jeans and needing release. I want to bury my cock so deep inside her, she won't know where I start or she ends. When her breathing returns to normal, I remove my fingers, lick them clean, and gently turn her over on my lap. Her hair is wet from sweat and is sticking to her forehead. I lean down and kiss her lips. She sighs, tasting herself on my lips as the fire released from her moments earlier builds again into a burning inferno with my tongue.

I want her lips around my cock, but my discipline is waning. I break our kiss. "On your knees, Wren."

She obeys and sinks between my knees to the floor. The sight of her sweaty, bound, and submitting to me releases the animal in me. I stand to remove the remainder of my clothing. She watches my movements intently, recording each step in her mind. I turn away, bending to remove the pants from my ankles. I rotate towards her and she gasps. My erection is throbbing as she stares her fill.

"I'm not sure that's gonna fit," she stammers, licking her lips as I fist my weeping cock from root to tip.

I see the juices dripping down her thighs and my hunger escalates.

"I want you now, Wren." My hands cup her elbows, lifting her eye-level with me as I spin and help her place her feet on the edge of the couch. I place her bound wrists above my head, connecting us.

"Bend your knees and spread your legs for me, Wren," I order and she obeys.

Her breathing quickens as I lubricate my dick by sliding back and forth through her juices, pleasuring both of us. I'm trembling, restraining so my Vampire strength doesn't hurt her. I have to be careful; she's human, and my true mate. Her body is burning for me, and only I can satisfy the longing she craves.

"Please, Aldin. I need to feel you inside me."

I gaze into her passion filled eyes, my future. "I want to possess and own every single inch of you, my Wren. Body, soul, and mind. The same that you have done to me."

I pledge my life to her.

I angle my cock at her entrance and slowly push forward, inch by excruciating inch. "You're so tight," I huff, continuing my short thrusts and needing her to take all of me. She starts to rock her body and I grab her hips, holding her in place. "Don't move. I'm barely controlling myself." I take a deep breath and growl. Her body is heaven, perfectly made for mine. We're two halves of a whole that form a magical bond, sealing us together for eternity.

A few small thrusts later and I'm bottomed out. Our pelvises meet and we are joined as one. No beginning and no ending, only my Wren and me.

"Lift your legs up and rest them on my hips. Lock your ankles and hold on," I demand urgently. My patience has ended and I need more of her.

She pants in my ear, her hands threaded in my hair as her pussy squeezes around my dick. A groan escapes my lips as I question, "Are you ready, my Wren?"

"Yes, sir."

I wrap my arms around her. The intimacy of watching her face as I slowly withdraw to the tip breaks my concentration and calls to the animal inside me. I begin hammering into her clenching muscles.

"Oh god, yes," she encourages me, digging her fingernails into my back and rolling her hips forward thrust after thrust. "Harder. More. I need more."

Primal instincts take over to claim my true mate as my fangs lengthen, scraping against her intoxicating pulse. The tension builds into pain. My hands curve up to her shoulders and I'm driving into her over and over. The need grows stronger and I'm lost in her sweetness.

"Oh, Aldin … I need to … I'm so close. Not going to last …" she huskily utters in rhythm with my entrance into her silky, warm body.

I blissfully mutter my response. "Not yet. Too good. Don't want to stop." The feelings she evokes, I don't want to end.

"Please," she exclaims, then sinks her teeth into my neck, biting hard and causing a chain reaction.

I wildly continue slamming into her clenching channel as my heavy balls start to tingle and draw up. I struggle for control as sweat drips in the space between our connected bodies. With my legs spread wide, aching for release, I growl in her ear, "Now, Wren. Come with me, now!"

Immediately her body convulses and her pussy pulses around my cock. "Aldin," she sobs, reaching the pinnacle of her pleasure. Quivers of ecstasy rack her body as my eyes zoom in on her drumming pulse, and the scent of sex fills the room.

Instinctively, I react, sinking my fangs into her neck and drawing her blood, her life source forever bound to mine. She is now a part of me. Mine. Pumping almost savagely, the blood rushes to my swelling cock, and her body spirals into a second climax from the endorphins released into her from the bite. The taste of her essence in my mouth and her convulsing tight muscles around my cock triggers my orgasm, milking every last drop of cum from me. I continue to revel in her taste when incoherent words of praise and satisfaction filter my sexually-induced trance.

The hunger and intense pleasure subsides as I become aware of what I have done. I retract my fangs from her and lick the two puncture wounds on her neck, sealing them instantly. Only another Enchanted Immortal can see them. By taking her blood, my fate is sealed to her for eternity. Even if she doesn't choose me, I will never again be with another woman. She is the only one my body will accept now.

She's boneless in my arms as I bite down on my tongue, causing blood flow, then kiss her, exchanging my blood for hers. I open her mouth and encourage her to drink. I give her only enough to replace what I took from her. She's oblivious to what happened and I won't complete the binding without her knowledge and acceptance. For now, I will wait.

Once I'm assured that she's taken enough of my blood, I ease out of her and adjust her limp body in my arms. Cradling the precious cargo, I pivot and walk down the hallway to find her bedroom. Her scent is strongest in the room on the right. Entering, I'm overwhelmed with emotions I haven't encountered before now. She's mine. She was made for me. The perfect light to my darkened soul. I have to protect her. She's vulnerable to others until we complete the ritual, bonding us as mates.

I need to leave soon. Wren's breathing evens out as she's wrapped securely in my arms after our night filled of passion. *No, that isn't right.* It was the most amazing sexual marathon I've had since

... ever. She gave me everything she had as I took everything I needed from her. Again, I can't help but think that we are perfectly matched for each other.

It is difficult for me to slip quietly away from this perfect woman ... *my true mate.* Shivering from the cold that has taken over my body, I can feel the sun coming up. It's time to get home and talk to Marcus. I steal one last glance at Wren, captured by the sight of her generous breasts moving up and down as she breathes in her deep, sated sleep. I leave her—content, for now.

# CHAPTER 10

## Wren

I ease my eyes gently open to the early morning sunlight filtering through the windows. My soul is happily singing from the previous night and early morning tryst with Aldin. Oh my goodness. My body begins to awaken, instinctively seeking out the man who caused my bliss. Turning my head, I gaze at the empty space on the other side of the bed and my heart races to my throat. A lump forms, causing a deep ache from the emptiness in my middle—something unfamiliar, foreign to me. I don't understand it. One night of ecstasy with Aldin and I'm hooked.

A single moonflower on the pillow is his goodbye. With a smile curling around my mouth, I carefully scoop the delicate bud up to my nose and sniff deeply. The fragrance explodes over my senses and I drift off to sleep again, dreaming of Aldin.

The next morning, I wake feeling well-rested. The clock by my bed says ten a.m. and my shift at the hospital starts in a few hours. I can't believe I slept twenty-four hours straight. I haven't slept that much since I was teenager. Guess Aldin wore me out. Stretching, I feel the pull of every muscle that was thoroughly fucked the previous night. Aldin was amazing. He was exotic, erotic, and dominant—just what I needed and craved. He was the total package and we were well-matched.

*Will I see him again? Was this just a one-night stand?* These thoughts race around my mind. I know that's what I was looking for in the beginning: hooking up and moving on 'til the next time I needed release. Now that I've had a taste of this man, I want more. I crave him. Feelings of love filter in and out of my head, and I can't shake the yearning to be near him. There was a defined moment when I knew I had been changed forever. I slipped across the line I swore to never cross.

"Well, shit," I mumble, realizing I didn't even get his number.

I stumble out of bed and open my door,

following the sound of music echoing off the apartment walls. The moment I arrive in the living room, I see Candie dancing around doing her exercises. Smiling to myself as she gives me her Candie-crazy face, she continues to dance and I move into the kitchen for the caffeine my body requires.

After I pour a cup of coffee and take my first sip, I almost orgasm from the rich, steaming flavor flowing around in my mouth. The tantalizing aroma of the dark roasted beans spin around me in the air. Taking another sip, I conclude that this is the best cup of coffee I've ever had.

"Hey, Candie. Did you make a new kind of coffee today?" I yell into the living room, hoping that she can hear me.

Candie saunters into the kitchen, sweat dripping down the sides of her face, and takes a seat at the bar as she takes a drink from her water bottle.

"What about the coffee, Wren? It's the same as always."

"Mmmm. It's delicious. Are you sure you didn't change it?" I ask again, curious, because every sip is nirvana.

"Nope. But if everything tastes better today, I

think it's the afterglow from a night of crazy sex and being knocked out for twenty-four hours, *girlfriend*." Candie laughs and exits, moving down the hall. "Gotta go shower, I have an early night at work! You'll have to give me every juicy detail when I get home later." She disappears behind her door.

I sit at the bar, contemplating her comments. It's true. I feel really good today, like I could run a marathon, and I haven't even finished my first cup of coffee. Maybe she's right. Maybe sex with Aldin was just what the doctor ordered. Fondly, I touch my neck, the lingering ghost of Aldin's lips and teeth grazing my skin causing a shiver down my spine and an aching in my lady bits.

There has to be a mark from all the sucking and biting. Tossing my hair to the side, I look in the mirror at the end of the bar. Nothing, nada. I move closer to get a better view, but there's nothing there. Crazy. I really thought I would be diving into my makeup kit to hide a hickey.

Giggling, I go shower. Duty calls. I need to go to the hospital for a few hours and make my rounds. I especially want to check on the miracle preemie baby Lana, and I know some patients will be discharging and I'll need to sign the paperwork.

Mentally, I make a to-do list for the rest of the day—and I add Aldin to it. I've got to find him. I have a burning need to see him again and that scares the hell out of me.

## *Aldin*

I made it home just in time to avoid the piercing sun on my back. Although my play time with Dr. Bishop was worth getting caught out in the early morning light, I chuckle to myself. Wren swamps my every thought. I can't believe I've found my mate and bound myself to her so quickly. I've joked over the years, saying I would never be good mate material and didn't want the ball and chain around my neck that comes with one. Clearly, I didn't know what the fuck I was talking about.

Mike greets me at the elevator as I head up to the penthouse.

"Morning, sir." Mike sniffs the air. "Smells like you had a good night." His chest rumbles deep within from his chuckle.

I pat his back, then nod and smile to acknowledge his comments. He knows I'm a man of few words. Riding the elevator to the top floor, I exit to go and find Marcus. My cell phone vibrates halfway down the hall. I glance at the caller ID and wince.

"Damnation." I realize my day is turning from really good to really bad in a matter of a few seconds.

Answering the call that I feel can only be bad news, I slide the bar across the screen.

"Agent Fox."

My voice sounds annoyed because he wouldn't be calling unless it was bad news. Agent Brenton Fox is an FBI agent and a hunter—not a hunter of animals, but of the supernatural. Fifteen years ago, we ran into each other. Literally. I was on the trail of a bloodthirsty Vampire and so was Fox. Long story short: I saved his life and he's owed me ever since. That night, he realized not all Enchanted Immortals are evil. In the end, it was a win/win for both of our kind. Fox watches my back and I do the same for him.

"Kovac," a gruff voice from smoking over the years spills through the line. "I put those feelers out like you asked and what I found out is some fucked up shit. According to wiretap transmissions and a few eyewitnesses, we've put together a timeline and a suspect. I've got people here who are freaked out and not understanding what's going on, Kovac. You've got to act on this fast. I have coordinates and maps I'm uploading now to your phone. It's a place to start." Agent Fox takes a deep breath and then releases the most disturbing part of his findings. "It's Jackson Parrish, Aldin. Fucker got away from us years back when you made the choice to save my sorry ass, and now he's out there killing more innocents." He pauses again and I feel the other ball about to drop. "Aldin, you need to watch yourself. Word is, he's also after you and Marcus. He wants what you have and is coming for you."

"Balls! I knew something wasn't settling right." I pause to compose the sharp, prickly anger rushing along my scalp. *Fucking Jackson.* He's a sadistic prick, haunting me with all his savage kills. "Thanks for the lead. We'll handle it. If you hear anything else..." I leave the rest hanging because it's already understood.

"If you need me, don't hesitate, Aldin. I've got your back. Later." With that last remark, Agent Fox hangs up.

After sliding my phone into my back pocket, I continue down the hallway to find Marcus. It's time to go hunting. A rogue who has escaped my grasp for fifteen years needs to be put down. And this time, I won't fail.

# CHAPTER 11

*Aldin*

Darkness has descended upon the city and it's early evening. The moon cascades through the unobstructed windows across the penthouse roof. We've been mulling over the maps and locations Agent Fox sent to me for hours. Tempers flare with the knowledge of the outcome. Either we find Jackson Parrish and destroy him, or more innocent people, human and Enchanted Immortals alike, will die.

"And you contacted the southern district?" Marcus asks wearily. He's frustrated and wants this to end, as do we all.

"Yes, my lord. I spoke with Esmerelda and she's worried. Three Vampires are missing. Two of the missing were younglings, newly made, just a few decades old. The other missing is a member who sits on their council. No one has heard from them." I explain to Marcus as my phone pings, indicating a message coming in.

"Here it is. She sent me a location that is suspect. I want to match it with what we already have to narrow down the search."

Walking over to the table full of maps, I find the point and put an X over it. A previous mark right next to the newest X confirms my suspicions. *We got him.*

Leaning over the table, Marcus delivers his final judgment. "We need to prepare. Call the enforcers home. We meet at dusk. Tell them to be ready to hunt. Make sure they know we will be preparing a celebration in honor of our impending victory. We feed. We hunt. We *kill*."

"Yes, my lord. It will be done," I rapidly reply and proceed in the direction of my office.

Once settled, I begin to make the necessary arrangements that will eradicate the world of a monster and his followers. First on the list are the Enchanted Immortals: Vampires, Shifters, Necromancer, and other supernatural beings. Marcus has formed many alliances over his centuries of existing. At the beginning, I believe he wanted to create a "family" of his own to aid in relieving his loneliness. It morphed into a network where thousands of Enchanted Immortals are protected from harm daily: safe places all around the globe for our kind, a shelter of sorts from the humans and other predators. I recall the stories he's told me of the death and annihilation of complete races that no longer exist because of the fear humans harbored of not knowing or understanding.

Over the centuries, hunters have claimed many Enchanted Immortal lives. Brenton Fox and I work together as Ambassadors, educating both sides, and a truce of sorts has been in place for the last fifteen years. Some of the elders will never accept it, but as long as Marcus reigns, no one will dare challenge his ruling, which is another reason of concern for him to leave me in control.

Next, I notify Agent Fox and his team. All are ready to go to war with us. I look up, rubbing the back of my neck when a flash of lightning fills the sky. It's midmorning and I've been working all night to ensure that everything goes as planned. I notice the black storm clouds moving in to darken the city, illuminated only by the occasional bolts of lightning in the distance.

I've been so caught up ensuring no detail was left to fate that I realize I haven't contacted Wren in over twenty-four hours. I scroll to Wren's phone number. While she slept, I called my phone from hers. Call me obsessed, but I had to have a way to contact her again. My mind is immediately reminded of the need burning deep within. Driven by that need, I finish up what I'm working on and rise to leave. On my way to the elevator, Marcus stops me.

"Where are you going, Aldin? The celebration is beginning. We need to feed well and be ready for the impending hunt."

I don't want to share my news about finding my mate or explain to him the feelings swirling around in my heart for the doctor just yet, so I play along and agree with him.

"Of course, my Lord. I wanted to clear my head, get some fresh air. I'm going for a ride and I'll be back later. Then, I will join you and the others in celebrating our anticipated victory over Jackson."

He pauses a moment to stare deeply into my eyes. I'm concerned my secret has been found out. The blood bond Marcus and I have shared over the years betrays me now by allowing him to read my emotions. Hell, it's not like I don't want to shout at the top of my lungs "I've found my mate!" but being so new, I've yet to deal with what's emerged between Wren and me. My trust in Marcus is unwavering. He is my lord, sire, and father.

He must find what he is searching for in my gaze. "Until later then, my son," he says before continuing toward the main room where the celebration is beginning.

I hastily move towards the elevator to exit. I don't look back. I worry that if I do, Marcus will stop and question me again. I will tell him when the time is right. I'm not ready to spill about my treasure. *Not yet.*

Once in the parking garage, I climb onto my Harley, rev the engine up, and peel out into the storming rain. Lightning flashes in the sky and the wind whips around me from the storm as I aim my bike toward the hospital. Pellets of water fall from the sky, but I have no need to worry about being drenched; my skin armor protects me and keeps me dry from the rain.

My need to see Wren is overruling my logic. Urgency taking hold of me to see my mate.

# Aldin's Wish

## *Wren*

Candie left for work and I went to the hospital. It was pouring rain outside when I arrived earlier in the day and, with a glance out of the window in my office, I notice the storm hasn't stopped yet. I've been thinking about Aldin and how I can find him when it hits me: He owns a brewery, but I just can't remember the name. I'll be stopping by to see Candie on my way home. 3:30 in the afternoon and that means only a few more hours and I'll know where to find him.

It's time for the last stop of my rounds today: baby Lana. I've been waiting for the results from the tests I ordered before examining her. They should be back by now.

I stand inside the prenatal ICU watching Lana sleep peacefully. I had already finished up the exam and, wow, this little girl is a trooper. She didn't even make a sound as I held her precious little body and rolled her around on the table, checking her from top to bottom. Adorable. Lana's blood and test results came back perfect.

She's a miracle.

Suddenly I'm struck with the familiar feeling of another presence assailing my surroundings, just like before. Turning around, I search for whoever is watching me.

Then I see him. Aldin is standing outside the room gazing inside, watching me.

*Whoa, wait a minute...*

Aldin smiles at me from the other side of the glass. I exit the room in a hurry to see him. I get the feeling deep down in my bones that something is different. Mysterious. Aldin's powerful aura radiates strength and comfort, calling to me, hastening my steps forward. We are connected and I've only known the man for a few days. A magnetic pull stirs deep emotions I have never encountered. What is happening to me? I shouldn't be obsessing for the next look or touch this man will gift me with.

His hypnotic gaze captures me and I'm reeled in to his open arms. His manly smell calls to my womanly desires and instantly I'm in need.

"Hello, my lovely Wren. I stopped by to see you. How is your patient, baby Lana, faring today?"

"She's a miracle. It was touch-and-go from the start. I'm so happy about her recovery. I was about to tell her parents she should be able to go home soon. I don't anticipate any problems in that little sweetie's future," I babble, placing my hands on his chest.

"Wonderful news. How are you feeling? I'm sorry I left before you woke, but I remembered a meeting and knew I couldn't get out of it. Did you like your flower?" he inquires, caressing my back.

"I did. How did you know moonflowers were my favorite? My mother always kept a bouquet on the dining room table." I smile at the fond memory from my childhood.

"I know many secrets about you, my lovely doctor," he quips.

My spine stiffens at his remark, and an uneasiness filters in my mind. That's odd. How could he know those details about me? Maybe Candie told him more about me than I expected. She normally doesn't give out my personal information. I have to remember to ask her about it later, mentally talking myself off the ledge.

He reaches for my hand and opens the door behind him, pulling me into a small closet, and quietly shutting us inside. The light trickling in from the crack at the bottom illuminates his face and I'm mesmerized by the desire burning in his stare. His embrace is solid as he nuzzles my neck, inhaling.

"I need you now, my Wren," he says, lifting the

skirt up my legs until his hand touches my inner thigh. I release a moan at the contact. "This is going to be quick, my lovely."

I don't care. I just want him to stop the ache growing inside of me. He guides me up against the wall, licking my neck in the same spot as he did the first time. He groans and nips me, causing a chain reaction to start inside my body, a flittering in my belly and pounding of my heart. Then he benches me straight up into a sitting position on his forearm, his strength a complete turn-on to my already charged body. I wrap my legs around his waist and lock ankles, anchoring me in place.

"You call to me, my heart. Every moment away from you, I longed to be back inside you."

His free hand unbuckles his pants and his already hardened cock extends forward. Grabbing the side of the delicate lace thong, he snaps the fabric, slides it into his pant pocket, and positions himself at my wet entrance, grinding his hips as his shaft slides back and forth on my channel priming him.

I clutch his shoulders and try to position him where I want him: right inside of me. He chuckles at my desperation and continues his leisurely assault on my pussy.

"Stop playing around and give me what I want, Aldin," I demand insistently. I know what I want and I want him now.

"Wren, I said quick not rough, my lovely. I want to savor every second, to remember later when you're not with me." He nibbles on my skin at his favorite place again. "You are so delicious."

The tingling sensation from his lips heighten my desire for him. He's playing with me and the thought of his dominant side causes me to shiver with need. I can't believe he is here with me. He's a *dreamsicle* on two legs, likeable, lickable, and definitely loveable. And, he's here with me. It all seems too good to be true.

"Aldin?"

"Hmmm."

"I'm really attracted to you. I can't seem to stop thinking about you. Do you feel the same about me?"

Huh? Word vomit. I didn't mean to ask him about my doubt.

He abruptly stops kissing me, looks directly at me, and with a broken voice tells me, "Before I met you, my Wren, everything I had done meant nothing. You are everything I never knew I was searching for and then more."

He gently lowers his lips to mine, and I'm lost in his passionate kiss, my doubts forgotten for now. He maneuvers my upper body and swiftly enters me with one thrust and stops, embedded inside. His cock throbs inside me.

He tears away from the kiss, looking at me. "What you do to me, my Wren ..." he feverishly mumbles.

He lavishes kisses down the column of my neck. A burning ignites in the bottom of my belly. He starts moving at a slow pace, causing my pussy to clench and tighten when he pulls back, not wanting him to leave.

In a deep husky voice, almost as an afterthought, he says, "We are two bodies, sharing one soul ... completing the other."

Suddenly, I'm flooded with an intense sensation of love and peace. I know somehow Aldin's words are responsible. The way I feel for him is an enigma. His strokes pick up momentum and I'm biting down on his shoulder to keep from screaming and alerting others to our activity in the hospital closet. A growl erupts from deep down Aldin's throat and I'm lost in the ecstasy he's creating. I use my inner thighs to ride him and he's hitting my clit every time he moves. I know the stimulation will have me climaxing soon.

"I'm so close," I whisper in between thrusts.

He lowers his mouth to my shoulder and bites the spot where I thought he had left a hickey before. The next second, I'm consumed with pain and then pleasure upon pleasure as I explode into bliss from Aldin's masterful strokes.

When my breathing returns to normal, Aldin is licking my shoulder. "You like the way I taste?" I ask with a laugh, catching him off-guard.

He stops and, after a few seconds, responds, "You are a delicacy I will never tire of, my Wren." Then, he lowers me to the floor.

He holds my waist while the feeling returns to my legs. I'm a little wobbly from the workout Aldin gave me. As soon as we are presentable, we exit the closet. I know I won't be able to look at that door again and not blush.

"I'm on my way to meet up with an associate of mine. Do you think I could take you to the theater Friday evening? I'll be tied up with my associate for the remainder of the day and into the evening tomorrow."

I clasp my hands together behind my back to stop the constant twirling. I've been doing it since I was a child when I'm nervous and I don't want him to notice the bad habit. Could he possibly have a family and he really isn't interested in me other than sex? Why do I feel so drawn to this man? How did my heart get involved so quickly? The doubts are beginning to overwhelm my consciousness, but then again, why would he ask me to the theater? It's another of my treasured pastimes my parents shared with me growing up. I smile as my inner woman stands up and takes a bow. He is the man of my dreams.

"Aldin, that sounds wonderful. I haven't been since my parents took me."

Well, ever since my dad was killed. It's been so long.

"I'll pick you up at seven, then?" he asks, staring me down with longing and desire.

My name is paged over the speaker and duty calls. I pause before answering, unsure if I should say more. "I'll see you then."

"Until then, my lovely Wren," he promises, bowing his head to my hand and applying a kiss to it.

I walk down the hallway, feeling his eyes on me. I sway my hips provocatively, tempting the beast once again and smiling to myself when I hear him groan, my body reacting to the sound. As I turn the corner, I hear his cell phone ring. I stop to listen because, okay, I'm nosey. But I need to know if he is involved with someone else or if it's just my overactive imagination playing games with me. Logically, Aldin is a walking, talking dream—a catch. How can he be unattached?

Or is he?

"Kovac here." He pauses. "Hello, dear Nubia. Yes. One more stop, and then I'm on my way home." His voice fades as the elevator doors close.

I'm left feeling shocked and hurt. I've allowed my heart to get involved, something I normally do not do. It happened so quickly, I didn't realize until I heard him talking on the phone the impact he's had on me. Who is Nubia and why is she at his home?

My phone starts beeping. I answer it as I walk towards the elevator doors.

"Dr. Bishop, I apologize," says the nurse through the phone. "You were paged accidently by one of the trainees manning the desk. Just wanted to let you know before you headed this way."

"Thank you," I respond, ending the call as I open the door to the stairwell to begin my descent to the garage level. I'm going to follow Aldin and see where he's going. Yes, I'm a bit obsessive right now. I need to know if he's got a girlfriend or wife, then decide if I'm just his next conquest—before things get out of hand and I lose myself totally in him. The gnawing feeling inside me is causing an unsettling reaction. In forty-eight hours, Aldin has changed my entire world. Meeting him at the bar, was a coincidence, right? Maybe, maybe not? Either way, I'm hooked and need answers. It's not rational or logical, the way he's planted himself deep inside my heart. The only way I will know what to do is to find out myself.

I've been relying on myself for years. No biggie. I got this.

# CHAPTER

## 12

*Aldin*

Wren has my desire exploding once again as she saunters down the long white hallway of the hospital. The iridescent lighting highlights her hourglass shape in the pencil skirt she's wearing as her hips sway back and forth, hypnotically entrancing me. I want her. The quickie we shared moments earlier isn't enough to sate my hunger. I will always crave her. *She's mine.* I groan when her scent filters my way, remembering her legs wrapped around me and hearing the slight hitch of her breath. I affect her, too. She must feel our connection growing.

Bonded mates are rare, and a male, once he's found his true mate, is a force to be reckoned with. Possessive and dominating, but at the same time would do anything to make his other half happy. The tug of an overwhelming magnet is pulling us together while gently knitting our souls into one. The tendrils are weaving steadily every time we are close. In the end, without each other, we will perish. If Wren rejects me, I will have nothing to live for, always missing the other piece to my soul. It is the strongest bond known: true love.

I've met thousands of people throughout my lifetime. Some, I've called friends. Others, acquaintances or employees. Finding my true mate has changed my life forever. I'm no longer adrift in the sea of life by myself. I have a partner with which to share my dreams, passions, and future. I'm surprised by the longing to finish the mating. Women come and go in the lifestyle I have chosen. I'm never one to stay after satisfying my body's passions, but when I held Wren in my arms that first night, I knew I would never be the same.

As I move towards the elevator, my phone begins to blare a ridiculous tune. "Hell's Bells, Satan's comin' to you, Hell's bells, he's ringing them now," echoes down the hallway from the phone. Mike the jokester dubbed it as "Marcus' ringtone" and I quickly answer before I have to listen to more of it. Marcus is concerned and he had Nubia call when I hadn't returned to Dalca Towers for the evening. I had politely explained to her I am running surveillance before the enforcers arrive later tonight and to inform Marcus I would be returning home soon. For him to have someone check up on me sets warning bells off. He must know something is going on. I don't want to worry him, but until I have my mate secure, I won't chance someone knowing and using it as leverage against us, especially with the impending war against Jackson Parrish and his cronies. As soon as I return, I've got to let him know what's happened. Putting it off is no longer an option.

I ease out of the hospital parking garage and head west as the sun begins to set, the rain long gone. Once on the freeway, I let go as the powerful machine zooms to my destination. The trees lining a concrete barrier whip from the swirling air as the roar of vehicles echo through the tunneled underpass. I want to put my eye on the building where Parrish is able to open the doorway. The briskness of the air soothes my worried mind and before long I'm calculating the impending battle, searching for the least possible route with no casualties of my people.

Stopping a few blocks away from Parrish's last

known doorway, I park my bike and walk the remainder of the way. The area is quiet except for the sound of a train passing nearby and the lone light blinks on as dusk finally surrenders to the night. Hugging the shadows, I creep around the back where an upper window is partially cracked and light is escaping. I sniff the area and the perfume of human and Enchanted Immortal blood assaults me. I battle a rage inside of me as the tendrils of my beast reacts. The yearning to destroy the ones responsible for causing the bloodshed is powerful. I know by the amount of blood permeating the air that the individuals are dead or dying.

Years of training resurfaces and, driven by instinct, I assume battle stance, lowering my fangs and drawing on my power. Cloaked, I maneuver nearer to the window for a better look. One of his soldiers summons the doorway and I follow. It's a revolving doorway allowing Enchanted Immortals access back and forth. The smells intensifies with each step I go.

I stop, unable to believe what is in front of me, sickened by what my eyes are seeing. Bodies, Vampire *and* human, are hanging from hooks as the blood drains into a vat below. Moans from the barely-living filter among them. A young fledgling strains against the protruding hooks in his arms and legs. I notice his fangs have been removed when he grimaces. The pain etched across his face has me in motion, only to be stopped by footsteps near the opening on the side of the cavern. Striding across the cavern floor is my nemesis, Jackson, followed by two of his henchmen.

"We need more bodies—preferably alive this time—if we are going to find what I need," Jackson demands.

"Yes, my lord," they respond in unison.

"At least a pair of each. An elder and his fledgling and a bonded pair, which is rare, would be best. Watch Dalca's clan closely. There are bound to be mated Enchanted Immortals he protects. And knowing I take what is his will only sweeten the revenge I have planned for my dear brother."

He cackles as his hands form a steeple and his fingers begin rhythmically tapping at the tips. He proceeds along the bodies, poking and prodding, examining the living vessels being tortured.

"Find me a pair and bring them to me. I want every possible soldier searching for what I need. My time is nearing and I require more before the exchange." He turns to exit and stops dead in his tracks.

He swiftly moves his head in the direction I had been only moments before, but I've already moved, aware he might sense something amiss in the room. I believe he won't be able to feel my presence because of my lineage, but one can never be too careful when in the presence of their enemy. I'm a powerful Vampire and can only be sensed by someone as old as Marcus. Shaking his head as if his mind is playing tricks on him, he strolls out the door followed by his men.

I sink back to the shadows, exiting through the doorway. There's nothing I can do to help the ones barely breathing. I'm torn because I save innocents from tragedies such as this, and I rationalize quickly that I could not save them and make it to safety before being caught. Sadly, their lives are at an end, and I must warn Marcus and the others. We do have mated couples and newly-created Vampires among many of our people. My Wren is unprotected as well. There's something not adding up. By my calculations, Jackson has only been an Enchanted Immortal Vampire for fifty or so years. What "exchange" does he mean? Is he turning more humans for his army? But, the most disturbing thought I have is, what in damnation does he mean by calling Marcus his dear brother?

# CHAPTER 13

*Wren*

Aldin is pulling out of the parking garage when I open the stairwell door. I move fast, weaving in and out of the tightly-packed vehicles to my car, clicking the remote, and sliding in to crank the machine. I've got to keep close to him or I'll lose him with all the evening traffic in the city.

Uncertainty isn't something I'm used to, and Aldin is causing me to doubt the logic I've built my life around. I'm not sure how to handle the situation. Aldin is different from anyone I've ever met. His confidence is contagious. I picture him sitting in a boardroom full of his peers, directing them as he sees fit, demanding perfection from those present, and praising when the job is done correctly. I'm drawn like a moth to a flame. He's causing me to wish for a life with a white picket fence ... a real home. Settle down? Me? Never. I'm not the settling type, but with him, I could actually see myself in a few years holding his child.

*Hold up! Is this the beginning of the crazy train?*

I shake from the nonsense swamping me and focus on what I'm doing. The thought of anyone else touching Aldin infuriates me. I have no claim on him, not really. Yet ... I don't want anyone else to have him. What the fuck is happening to me? I think back to the events leading up to now. Overworking at the hospital earlier this week, sensing the man in the ICU, that same feeling happening again the next day while I was napping, then at the bar meeting Aldin ... could he have been the one I felt each time? When we made love, I know something happened.

The fog lifts as I rub my neck. Flashes of pain and pleasure overwhelm me. A glimpse of Aldin's face the minute before my orgasm plays in my mind, and I suck in my breathe suddenly, recalling the memory.

His eyes ... his teeth. *Holy shit!* I must've been dreaming. Maybe that's not what happened. But subconsciously I know I'm not dreaming, and he did bite me. What does this mean? I need to know. Did his bite cause the intense emotional turmoil I'm suffering now? I should be scared out of my mind, terrified that he is a psycho or—oh god, Hannibal Lecture's protégé—and he's going to eat me for dinner, right? For some ungodly reason, I'm not. The knowledge and answers I seek are parked just on the edge of my mind, waiting to be released. I can feel it as if it's something really important or life-changing swirling around in my soul. Aldin Kovac holds the key.

I follow Aldin through the crowded streets with horns blaring and red and yellow tail lights flashing by as he glides in and around the traffic effortlessly. I maintain a good stalking distance, just in case he realizes he's being followed. Once on the freeway, it's easier to maintain my covert operation. *Covert? Like Mission: Impossible. Haha! Who am I kidding?* My nerves are shaking my body and it's becoming hard to steady the wheel. The memory is replaying over and over in my head. I must remain in control. This is too important. Finding out more about Aldin will determine my next step. Possible heartache? Definitely, if there is someone else. Is he married? Is he *other*? Or am I wrong about everything? Am I delusional? Suffering from the same sickness my mother was locked in an asylum for?

When Aldin came to visit me at the hospital earlier, I was shocked, yet eager to see him just the same. There is an extreme pull between us, one that I can't deny yet don't quite understand. My body craves him and him alone. Even after one night, my mind is melding to the idea of keeping him all for myself—a sensation I'm unfamiliar with and at the same time secretly longing for.

I watch as Aldin exits onto an offramp at the south of town. I continue my pursuit. A few moments later, he pulls across from an abandoned warehouse. I trail slowly, parking in an alley with just enough sight to see him climb off his bike. Staring motionless into the darkness that surrounds me, I catch a glimpse of Aldin moving up to the rickety windows, peering in. What does he see? What is he looking for? The flood of questions boggle my overactive imagination. At the same time, a tsunami of desire ratchets down my spine and pools in between my legs just from seeing him across the quiet street. *Damn it, Wren, get it together. This is not the time nor place.*

I gain control of my faculties and move to exit my car quietly. My heart races like a stampede of a thousand horses. Aldin turns towards me as if he senses my presence. I hold my breath tightly, willing my whole self to be invisible while chanting inside my head over and over, *"I'm invisible. I blend in. I'm invisible. I blend in."* I build a barrier between our physical bodies in my mind so he will not see. Still as a statue, I wait for him to move on. I watch as he disappears to the back of the building, out of sight. *Thank god it worked.* After a few more beats of holding my breath and not moving a muscle, he appears from the shadows. His face is a mask of disgust and horror. He moves to his bike and cranks it up, departing the dark, sketchy area, and leaving me to uncover what he's hiding from me. My interest is piqued. What will I find?

Cautiously, I approach the abandoned building, going right up to the same window Aldin peered into moments ago. The glass panes are smudged with years of grime and gunk, making it difficult to see through. I pull my jacket sleeve down, gripping it in my hand and using it to smear some of the filth away, but the glass remains smoky and dense. I can't see anything.

A sound from behind has me twisting around to face three unsavory thugs. *Stupid, Wren!* I was so focused on getting answers, I totally forgot about the danger of being here in this part of town. As they inch closer with their arms spread wide, trying to cage me in, I notice their eyes are solid red. *Déjà vu.* I'm back in college experiencing the horrible attack all over again, and once again, nobody is around to help me.

"Stay away from me," I yell, stumbling backwards against the window and falling onto my ass. Scrambling out of their reach, I'm almost on my feet again when a hand grabs and twists my arm behind my back, jerking me against a solid body.

"What do we have here, gentlemen?" a new voice says from behind me.

I try to glance behind me, but the grip around my neck tightens, and then my world goes black.

# CHAPTER 14

## *Aldin*

Striding across the marbled floor entrance from the elevator, I'm met by the congregating team of Enchanted Immortals and Hunters ready to descend onto Jackson. Their faces are grim with determination, and vengeance laces many who have lost loved ones that suffered by his hand over the last decade. We will end their suffering and remove the world of his evil ways.

Marcus is standing in the center when he notices my arrival. "Aldin, we weren't sure if you would be joining us tonight," he remarks with a hint of sarcasm and concern mixed together. *He knows ...*

"My lord, I've news that will help ensure our victory. I come from seeing with my own eyes the

**123**

wickedness and depravity Jackson has inflicted upon Enchanted Immortal and humans alike. He is evil and must be destroyed."

I've caught the attention of everyone in the room. Voices are quiet and movement stops. Marcus nods in affirmation for me to continue.

"The place we believed he resides in is definitely his latest tomb of torture. The doorway is open. I witnessed the horrendous acts he is practicing and it must be stopped. Bodies hanging on the walls being drained of blood while the beings still live. His doorway isn't guarded by enchanted wards, so I was able to follow an Enchanted Immortal cloaked. Jackson has surrounded himself with an army of brainless bodies as his protection. Most likely he is controlling their every move, a grand puppeteer."

"What do you mean, draining blood?" Marcus asks, shocked at the prospect. His body is tense with an awareness of the act.

"A fledgling was secured on what I took to be meat hooks while his blood drained into a vat of sorts. His fangs had been removed and he was still alive. I wanted to help him, but Jackson showed up and I had to retreat. I didn't want to give him the chance to sense my presence."

"Hmmm. Tell me more, Aldin. Every detail is important." Marcus spouts question after question, expecting immediate answers. "What else? Smells? Lights? Noises? How were the bodies positioned?"

I think back to the surroundings and begin to remember the smallest of details. "The lighting was dim but lit by four large black pillar candles located in each corner of the large space." I close my eyes and inhale. "At first it didn't register over the strong scent of blood and decay, but yes, I'm positive I smelled a hint of lavender and resin."

"And?" Marcus anxiously prods for me to continue.

"Each body was positioned in a line between the candles exactly the same distance apart with a silver flashing placed below attached to a gutter angling into the center vat. The vat collecting the blood was located in the center, a large obsidian stone hung above. It glowed bright red whenever a drop of blood dripped into it."

"Impossible," Marcus exclaims, interrupting my dreary recollection. No longer standing still, he's pacing the length of the room mumbling to himself over and over. "No. I never believed he could escape. This cannot be happening again. He was banished into a lamp, never to be released, and imprisoned within the tomb of Czar Nannook in another realm, never to be awoken."

"Who was? My lord, what are you saying?" I cooly inquire.

The entire room has grown eerily quiet, tight with anxiety of the news Marcus has about the monster we are hunting.

"Pure evil, Aldin. Evil like no one has ever known. So many lives were lost. The Immortal Conflict was fierce, and only the oldest Immortals lived to see a new day, and every one of them succumbed to the black magic he yielded." His eyes grow distant as he continues his gruesome tale. "Only my sisters and I share the knowledge of the location. We are the only Immortals alive that know where the enchanted tomb is. I haven't shared that secret with anyone. Not even you, my trusted son. I was waiting for the right time to share the burden with you."

I'm stunned by his words. All these years, he has trained me to take over his kingdom and lead the Enchanted Immortals, and I have never heard anything about a tomb or Immortal Conflict. You would think with all the preparations he was making for me to assume his role, he would have felt that the background about our race almost not existing would be important to know. How did they keep this so quiet? Our historians are adamant about the records they keep. Some are fanatical to a point of absurdity. A few I've met are argumentative and not so pleasant. My heart pounds loudly from the news Marcus has bestowed upon us.

Every new Enchanted Immortal is recorded in the "Forever Living Enchanted Immortal" scroll. The scroll is a divine entity, all-knowing. When a new Enchanted Immortal is created, a name and date is immediately burned on to it. Whether it's a Necromancer or Shifter, naturally-born or other, a name and date appears. Every Enchanted Immortal throughout time is listed. If one meets their death, a new date appears. The scroll is kept in a temple at the center of the Enchanted Immortal Kingdom, accessed through a doorway in Egypt guarded day and night. I've seen it once when Marcus showed me that my own name had been added. It's a sacred bonding between a master and offspring.

For a brief moment, excitement strums through my body. I will be traveling to Egypt with Wren for the bonding ceremony, once she accepts our blood bond. I wonder how she will accept all the changes. From my interactions with my Wren, she is a very logical human. Gifting her with this knowledge will need to be executed delicately. She's human and life as she knows it will end. Humans will age, but not Wren; she will be tied to my life source.

"This changes nothing. We banished him once and we will banish him again. We are strong and must stop him." Marcus vehemently declares.

Startled, I try to catch up with him. "I'm at a loss. Who must be banished and why, my lord? I thought we were hunting Jackson Parrish and now you say we aren't?"

"A monster, Aldin. Someone I hoped never to see again in my eternity of living. He's known as Baako, God of the Night Realm. He captures souls of the lost and tortures them for eternity. He lives off their pain and suffering."

Agent Fox comments, "Some of the scrolls passed down by hunters, generation to generation, have mentioned a boogeyman of sorts from the beginning of time. Are you saying this Baako is the one?"

"Yes." Marcus nods and shakes his head back and forth as if reliving a horrible nightmare. "One in the same. He is using Jackson as his living vessel to perpetuate his rising. He needs a body to replace the one he is currently using. His soul lives in this realm while his body is entombed in another realm under strong protection wards."

The eerily quiet room begins to hum with fear and uncertainty. For Marcus to lose his calm persona and react the way he has unsettles even the oldest Immortal. Fox and his men are huddled together, whispering. I'm at a loss with their need to whisper the conversation; don't they realize we can hear them?

"Fox, repeat what you are saying for everyone's benefit, please," Marcus calmly directs.

He shuffles from foot to foot nervously. "We are concerned, Marcus. If you feel he is so powerful and, well ... you're Marcus, King of the Enchanted Immortals ... how are we possibly going to defeat him? The history books mention a blood cleansing, but with no instructions or guidance. Nothing we could use. We believe contacting the twins, Jazmine and Jada, is our only hope. Do you think they would know of this? They are the only Immortals powerful enough to conjure a vanquishing spell against Jackson. You said he's a god? How would that work?"

"Tricky." Marcus furiously ponders Fox's

comments as his hand runs through his short hair. "I'm not sure I want to bother them just yet. They prefer to live in seclusion. Large crowds bother them. They haven't been seen by anyone in many years. But, I will go and request their help. When they learn of the body-jumping of Jackson Parish, I am more than positive they will want to help."

"This is a life-changing event, Marcus. Without their help, we could all be facing a grim future … possibly no future at all. You have to try," Fox gently says.

"Yes, I know you're correct, even understand your concerns. The situation is out of my hands with Aldin's new revelation. Seems I have no choice but to summon them to help. We will await their arrival and expect all to go well once they are among us."

## *Marcus*

I exit the elevator onto the basement level. As I walk down the long pristinely white hallway to my vault, my mind goes back to everything Aldin recalled.

"Such a mess. After all these years, he's still learned nothing."

Standing outside the vault, I place the combination into the pad and the door slides open. I step in as the door seals behind me. The chamber I've entered has two physical doors. One on the right is tarnished and brass-colored—an earth doorway. Open it and wish to be anywhere on earth, and it will take you there. The door on the left is silver with gold trim, and it is much different and sacred. This doorway can lead to other realms in the universe, but only an original Immortal can open it.

I begin to speak the spell of old, ordering the silver doorway to be opened. Bright lights flash as the solid door liquefies into clear, shimmering waves. I walk through to the other side and greet my beloved sisters.

"The time is nearing, my sisters. The prophecy foretold has been triggered. He has found his mate. We must be ready. Your assistance is required from this point forward."

"We are ready, my dear brother," Jada hastily responds.

Jazmine sadly sighs. "Let us begin our quest."

# CHAPTER 15

*Aldin*

The exchange of doubt and hope among those in the room continues once Marcus leaves on his errand to summon the magical twins. I've only been privy to seeing the beautiful creatures once, and that was at a distance. In the past, Marcus deemed their privacy and protection absolute, never allowing interaction with them as a possibility for anyone, human or Enchanted Immortal alike. For him to agree to disturb their sanctuary of peace reiterates the drastic circumstances developing for Enchanted Immortals.

Wren's mortality as a human enters my thoughts. I'm filled with unease, knowing she is out there without my protection. Existing without her now after what we have shared would destroy me. I now understand why, after all these years, Marcus is unable to move on. I need to speak with Marcus when he returns and plans need to be made for integrating her into the Enchanted Immortal way of life. Explaining the differences between us won't be easy. I'm not sure how she will react. I've marked her and, for me, there is no turning back.

I'm so focused on Wren's protection when a sense of urgency and pain grabs ahold of me. I collapse to the marble floor, writhing in pain and clutching my chest.

"Aldin, what's wrong?" Strong arms try to hold me still as I continue to squirm in agony on the floor.

"Help him." I hear Brenton yell, and footsteps move closer to where I'm lying on the cold marble floor.

Blood rushes faster as my chest pounds harder from the adrenaline coursing through me. *What's happening to me?* All of sudden, I'm whimpering. Again, emotions swamp me that are so unfamiliar. An overwhelming fear and helplessness bathe my entire being. Desperation claims me followed by total blackness.

Darkness envelops me as I spin down a

cavernous hole. The never-ending feeling of rapidly descending into nothingness pummels me. My arms and legs are melded against the trunk of my body, unmovable. After a moment of being unsure of how much longer I will have to endure the endless falling, I suddenly stop.

Voices. I hear voices far away as I struggle to open my eyes. Blinking away the fogginess, I strain to focus on the shapes taking form in front of me and am startled when Jackson Parrish and another Vampire appear.

"She is his mate and carries his unborn son, Jafar. The first original Immortal conceived since the Conflict. A descendant of the almighty Marcus Dalca is in my clutches. She is the key to destroying him once and for all." Jackson's evil laugh echoes in the cavern.

"Yes, your majesty, but how did he get around the curse? How did he know?"

"They've found a way to circumvent the blasted curse, the same way I've been reborn over the centuries, I'm sure. If you hadn't been linked to me, I would be stuck in that realm for eternity."

Jafar reminds him, "And, after all these centuries of searching, we still haven't found the doorway to your tomb. It's protected by a powerful ward. If their power is weakened, I should be able to pinpoint a location within a hundred mile radius of the doorway. The last time, we were so close. Do you believe this is the reason the twins' location is kept a secret?"

"Yes. Marcus' plan is crafty, but not foolproof. Regardless, we will make plans now for the sacrifice and exchange. Everything is in place. Even the planets are aligning that will help boost my powers. I've waited centuries to claim my rightful throne. The throne my beloved brother stole from me. He will pay dearly for the pain and suffering he has caused me. Beginning with his precious creation, Aldin. Once, my body is released from the tomb and my soul is reunited, I will be unstoppable."

My eyes travel around the cavern and land on something that sends me exploding with anger, losing my prided self-control. *My Wren!* She is floating midair, her long auburn hair unbound down her spine with her head hanging back. Her clothes from earlier have been replaced with a sheer white garment, baring her beautiful body for all to see. A foreign ache starts in my gut at the possibility of losing my mate. I notice her chest moving and calm slightly, knowing she's alive. My eyes check her body for any harm and end on her angelic face, and I'm shocked at what I find. Blue eyes focused and staring intently at me. I inhale trying to catch her scent, and can't.

My body is yanked backwards, spiraling towards my ascension, Wren's body fading rapidly from my sight. "No," I vehemently scream, fighting to return to her, only to have my arms and legs not listen to my demand.

"Aldin?"

My body is shaking profusely.

"Wake up, Aldin," a strong voice demands.

I recognize that voice.

"Aldin, I command you to obey me now."

I must obey him. My subconscious won't allow me to ignore his command. Willing my eyes to open, I am comforted at what I see. I'm in my bedroom laying in the middle of my large platform bed, which is centered in the room. The concerned expressions on their faces show. Marcus and the twins surround me.

Looking directly in his eyes, I try to relay the anguish and turmoil at what I saw.

"Marcus ... Wren," I weakly mutter. "Help her," I manage to say before blackness consumes me again.

# CHAPTER 16

## *Wren*

Hundreds of small flames illuminate the darkness, casting shadows on the walls in the large hollow cavern somewhere in the middle of nowhere. I don't know where "here" is, even though I've been trying to remember how I got from the warehouse to here. A powerful force within me beckons for me to listen. I've been ignoring the pull on my consciousness for some time now, even though time is irrelevant in this place. I've been counting the drops from the moisture that has built up from over the years to stop the insanity trying to take a hold of my mind. *How long is forever?* I wonder. Then I answer myself: one second more of enduring this craziness. Have I gone mad? Maybe.

Two rather young, good-looking men—one claiming to be a vampire and the other the god Baako—have been discussing the end of the god Maarku, enacting revenge from eight hundred years ago, and Baako claims to be the rightful heir of the throne for Immortals gods.

Yeah, right, I've got two tickets on the loony bin train for these bozos.

Yet the tugging in my mind won't let the reality of what they are saying go. Awareness occurs when I realize I'm able to understand the conversation the two vampires are having even though I know they are not speaking English. It sounds similar to Dr. Kalile's native language and he is from Egypt.

This must be a dream even though it feels so real. Strange things are going on right before my eyes. I'm Alice in Wonderland and I've fallen down the notorious rabbit hole with no way back. *Holy Fuck!* I know I'm hallucinating because Aldin is here now. I've been trapped within my own mind, dangling in the middle of this cave, butt-ass naked except for the sheer white drapery wrapped around me. I'm not cold or hot. I don't feel anything.

"Wait." Aldin begins drifting backwards towards the light. "I need you. Please don't leave me here," I silently beg. The words never escape my lips, and then he's lost from my sight.

I'm alone again. Drifting. *Aldin, where are you? Aldin, I need you,* I chant endlessly, willing him to return to me. Time has no meaning.

An all-too-familiar feeling wraps around my consciousness. *Aldin.* I'm sure I feel his presence with me again, but this time I can't see him. Invisible arms surround me, comforting me in the shadowy abyss. He's back.

"My lovely Wren. I am here. I will protect you and our unborn son." Aldin speaks clearly inside my head as if he's sitting right next to me whispering in my ear.

"Aldin, thank god. You heard me. Felt me calling out to you. You're here. Wait, what the fuck did you just say? Our child? Unborn son?"

Aldin's gentle laughter permeates through me causing me to forget my question for a moment.

"Yes, my Wren. You are carrying our son. It is true. There is much I need to tell you. I didn't want to explain to you like this, but it seems who I am will have to be told." I feel the sadness of Aldin's emotions as if they were my own. I sense the truth behind his words, but I can't believe it. It's not logical.

"*Okaaay* ... So, explain," I ask, unsure.

Aldin sighs. "Oh, my Wren. What I'm about to tell you will change your life forever."

A half psychotic laugh permeates through me. "As if stating that I'm having a baby and being held in stasis in this strange place is not life-changing already? Not likely. This has to all be a dream. A really strange dream in which I don't know the outcome yet. Just spill it, Aldin," I demand with a condescending edge in my voice.

As if he's shaking his head Aldin continues. "I am what my people call an Enchanted Immortal Vampire, one of three races created eons ago by the gods to protect humans and the Earth. There are Necromancers, people of magic. Shifters, who can take the form of any living being. And Vampires, like me, guardians of the night. I was created over two hundred years ago in the year eighteen twenty."

He pauses. Rationally, I cannot seem to grasp what he is telling me. My dreams usually give way to warnings. Am I being warned to stay away from Aldin? Or is he the missing piece in my life? It's all too crazy.

"This is very real, Wren. I assure you," Aldin says, as if he heard my musings. "When I get you out of here, we will have this conversation again."

"Alrighty, big boy. If you say so. But what does all this have to do with me? You're telling me you are an Enhanced Immortal."

"*Enchanted* Immortal," he corrects me. "You are my true mate, my Wren. You must feel the connection between us growing. Pulling us together. A force stronger than either one of us. I knew it the moment I saw you in the neonatal unit at the hospital, when I came to help save my niece."

"It was you? I felt something in the room with me. I thought I was going insane, but it was you? And what do you mean by true mate?"

I tell myself this can't be happening as I slip further down into the rabbit hole.

Our exchange is cut off from voices coming into the cavernous vault.

"Are you sure, your Majesty? Can this be possible?" the one called Jafar asks.

"It's brilliant, my old friend. I felt a part of Maarku within the womb. I'm certain now this is how he unlocked the curse," the god Baako answers.

All at once, I feel the pull like tugging on both ends of a Twizzler taut until it snaps in two. Aldin is leaving me again. "Please Aldin. Stay. Don't leave me alone."

There is no answer. I have to wake up. I'm over this fantasy. *Wake up Wren! Wake up!* Nothing. The voices in the cave capture my attention again.

"I can be reborn into an Immortal. And the need to find my original body will be nonexistent. The son she carries will be my host. Once again, I will be all powerful," Baako boasts. "The best part will be defeating my brother Maarku once and for all and taking away everything he loves and holds dear ... again."

Evil laughter explodes around me and my heart jumps to my throat in terror. No. This cannot be happening. If what he is saying is true, he plans on taking the baby's soul that I'm supposedly carrying. Since I'm in this delusion with no way out, I can't let that happen. Even if I wake up and it's all been a dream. In the real world, I always take care of my own.

# CHAPTER 17

*Aldin*

Strong emotions I can't identify shake me to the core. Whispering captures my attention and, with as much effort as I can muster, I focus on what's being said. Unlike before, I can't open my eyes. They aren't paying attention to my weak plea. It's as though all bodily functions have shut down except my brain. I'm thinking clearly and trying without any success to move. I'm alive and unharmed, but restrained. That's odd. Something being said draws me back. The word "mate" is mentioned. Who are they talking about?

"He's traveled far away from us. Possibly another realm," a soft feminine voice says.

Something is nagging me. It's right on the edge of my mind, but I can't recall what it is.

An identical feminine voice coming from the opposite side of the room. "He will need nourishment to regain his strength from one of us, now that we have temporarily severed the bond. The bond is strong between them. Something is drawing on his life force. Her magic is awakening and the stasis her body is in calls to him."

What magical awakening? What nourishment? I shouldn't require blood now. I have my mate's blood surging within.

"I'm afraid his memory will return soon as well. The spell will only last long enough to replenish him and help secure his mind for the melding," Marcus sadly comments near me.

The smell of blood jolts me from my lumbering as my teeth sink into a willing donor. The moment the delicious taste hits my tongue, I know Marcus is providing his blood for me. The hold from earlier is gone also. I open my eyes to see Marcus watching me with a sadness I've never seen before.

"You are my son, Aldin. Never believe differently. I choose you," he earnestly declares.

Finishing, I pause to lick the wound on his arm and acknowledge him. "And you are my father." I can tell my words have a powerful effect on him. I move to sit up and I am met with two sets of identical green eyes. The twins are even more beautiful than I remembered: long, sun-kissed strands of hair frame their round faces.

Twin smiles forms on lips the color of blood as they simultaneously speak: "You had us worried, young one. Thank the gods you returned from your slumber."

"I'm not sure what has happened while I was gone, but thank you for your kind words, your royal highnesses." I nod, acknowledging both before I ask, "Marcus, what in the hell is going on? The last thing I remember is falling on the floor, overwhelmed with the emotions channeling within me. I'm almost certain the emotions came from a young one, an infant, maybe. Then I was wrapped in protection only a mother's womb provides while growing. Puzzling, isn't it? I'm not sure what I was a part of."

"More than you are aware, my son. The finishing touches of a long ago foreseen plan to right the wrongs of an overzealous god is falling into place." Marcus pauses, lost in his memories. "Quite puzzling, indeed. The transference can happen, but only with a creation of the god Maarku's bloodline. An ancient prophecy tells of a blooded unborn reaching out for help from the womb to his parents. I sense there is something you want to tell me. Am I right, Aldin?"

"Yes. That is correct, my lord. I was waiting for you to return from your errand, my lord. I wasn't looking and thought I would never find one. The possibility only fleetingly entered my mind. I was sure the three wishes granted by you would be all I was allowed in an eternity. Once again I am wrong because fate had something more in store for me. I have found my true mate."

"The time is upon us. The prophecy has begun." Marcus directs his statement to the twins and they nod in agreement.

"Yes, it is time. We have waited eons for you, Aldin," Jazmine excitedly says.

Jada clarifies, "Yet in human years, only eight hundred have gone by."

I look at the three Immortals standing before me and notice the resemblance not only in appearance, but the regal posture each possess. How had I missed this before when I was in their presence? They are naturally born and have seen the worst and best over the years. The wisdom radiating among them comforts my jumbled feelings.

"You've mentioned a prophecy twice now, my

lord. What are you referring to? I do not recall any mention of a prophecy in our history."

"I had hoped this day would never come, but it appears I can no longer keep this part of history from you. What I'm about to tell you will change your perspective forever. I apologize in advance but I must place an enchantment on you." He pauses, waiting for my nod of acceptance.

I bow my head immediately, acknowledging to him that I agree. "Your will, my lord."

Marcus places the binding: "By my command, you are never to speak of this again to anyone, whether by choice or force. If by force, you will not be able to remember. It will vanish from your mind and you will not be able to betray me. If by choice, your lips will seal and your voice will be lost for all time. So let it be said, so let it be done."

I straighten and wait for his story to unfold.

He doesn't waste any time before he starts. "At the dawn of time, there were two Immortals, the god Zenon and his mate, the goddess Augusta. They had three children: the eldest son Baako, a daughter Jadzia, and the youngest son Maarku. For thousands of years, peace reigned over the realms under their leadership with humankind."

Jazmine's soft voice continues where he left

off. "Their love was renowned for each other and their subjects, but most of all, their children held their hearts. When Baako became restless and desired more than all that he had been given, Zenon and Augusta decided to create the Enchanted Immortals. Three new races: Necromancer, Shifters, and Vampires. A new race representing each child of the gods. The new companions the gods were given to oversee with the understanding the new races would be guardians of Earth and all who dwelled there."

"What began as a gesture of love," Jada explains, "quickly turned into something evil when the eldest son, Baako, introduced dark magic. Baako's desire for power became humankind's worst enemy. By calling on the power of the Abgrund Stone, Baako began to practice the art of body snatching. For a brief time, the horror stories known today of killings and death of supernaturals and humans took place. The darkest moment was when Zenon and Augusta realized Baako's actions had to be stopped."

Marcus nods and continues. "After he was questioned by his parents, Baako devised a hideous plan to capture them in an alternate realm with no doorway home, lost to all who loved them. When the Immortal Conflict began, Zenon and Augusta were caught off-guard and trapped, leaving Jadzia and Maarku behind to find a way to stop their brother. Jadzia concocted a powerful enchantment to capture Baako inside a lamp for eternity and bury the lamp inside a tomb. Maarku found the realm and cast wards up to keep it hidden. Unfortunately, Baako had help from one of his followers who was able to sever his soul from his body just as it was being cast into the realm, assuring Baako the ability to body-jump for eternity ... unless he can locate his body."

"So why are you telling me this, Marcus? I don't understand what this has to do with me."

"You are the one we have been waiting for, Aldin. You have initiated the prophecy by finding your true mate."

"I'm confused. What does the prophecy have to do with me?"

"Jadzia knew they would each have to give a part of their essence to bind the enchantment, which would then be reincarnated into a human. They had to bide their time. You, Aldin, are the human who received Maarku's essence. You are the key to ending Baako's terror once and for all. You are truly my son, Aldin. You carry a part of me inside of you. I am the god Maarku."

I'm taken back at the revelation that Marcus is a god and a part of him has been merged with my spirit. All this time, he has been walking among us—a god—and I didn't even know. Struggling to remember something important tugging at my subconscious, I'm flooded by the memory of Wren and my son.

"Marcus, I have a son! How is that possible?" I cry out.

Marcus grabs Jada and Jazmine's hand, smiling. "It is the prophecy, Aldin. We are so close to seeing them again."

# CHAPTER 18

*Wren*

I'm floating in a bubble of liquid goo. I can breathe. How is this possible? I'm encased inside a cocoon of warmth. Or maybe it's all just another part of this fantastical dream state that I'm in. The impressions of happiness and contentment flood my senses. Am I waking up? *Finally ...*

Opening my eyes, I stare at the concave rock walls dripping all around me. *Fuck!* I'm going crazy. Yep. Just like my mother. This can't be reality. *Damn it, Wren, you're a doctor for god's sake!* Think.

Everything Aldin confessed to me, I replay over and over in my mind. Enchanted Immortals? True mates? What reason does he have to lie, if this is real? That's the million dollar question. The connection he talked about is undeniable. I feel it too. Can I trust that this is real? I really have gone off the deep end, thinking such things. I need a sign, something that makes all of the chaos concrete. Right?

Strong emotions encompass me as my belly starts to flutter. What the fuck? Somewhere deep inside me, I already know the answer.

Giving in to the dream, I say in my mind, "Hello."

Pleasure. Jubilation. The stirring of another intertwined with my soul causes a restlessness within me, only to be instantly replaced with peace.

It's not Aldin. This is very different. Can it be real? Is it ... my son? Okay, so I've truly lost it. But who the fuck cares? This is my dream, right?

"Hello, little man. I'm your mommy." I giggle as affectionate laughter fills me. I jump in with both feet. "Don't you worry, little baby Aldin." I feel another flutter. "You like that, don't you? Haha! Well, I won't let anything happen to you, baby. Your father is coming for us ... I hope."

Another evident form of empathy flows around me—feelings of hope, along with protection. Already, my baby is fierce. I love it.

"We need to call your daddy, baby Aldin. I

chanted and wished for him before and he came. Maybe I can do it again. If you can understand me and I believe you can, help me, baby Aldin."

Again, the flutter within comes, and I smile. Let's do this.

"Aldin, we need you. Aldin, please come. Aldin, we need you. Aldin, please come."

The air turns heavy and those ominous feeling return. Aldin.

"He's here, baby Aldin. We did it."

"My lovely Wren, I'm here. Are you well? Our son? I've been out of my mind with worry. I don't know how long I'll be able to stay with you this time, but know this: we are coming for you and our son. Marcus now has your location."

"Aldin, we're scared, but for now we're alright. Baby Aldin is quite the little guy."

Aldin's deep electric laughter blankets me, and for a brief time, all is right.

"He is quite special, as are you, my mate."

"Whoa, buddy. First, you have to tell me what that means. You got yanked away before you were able to tell me."

"Yes, my Wren. I will explain as much as I can. A true mate is the other half that makes a whole, a bond so strong and fierce that one can't live without the other. It's love in its purest form and you are mine."

No. This can't be. I swore long ago that I would never be like my parents. I would never succumb to one person and take a chance of being alone one day, going crazy if the other person left or died. I just can't. But what if I lose my one chance of happiness? Aldin is my dream guy, everything I could ever want and more. If all of what he says is true, baby Aldin will need his daddy. I can't or won't keep him from his child.

"This is all so overwhelming, Aldin. So irrational." Palpitations begin in my belly and flutter to my heart.

"Ah, my precious mate," Aldin murmurs. "It will take time to understand all that you have learned and seen in such a short period. I can wait as long as it takes for you to grasp it all. I would do anything for you and our unborn son, my Wren. But just know this, my Wren: In the end, you will be mine."

"You say all the right things, my Aldin," I teasingly joke.

Chuckling, Aldin continues, "You are worth it. As I told you before, we will have this conversation again, Wren, once you and our son are safe."

I'm immersed with affections of love and happiness swaddling around me, inside of me, and through every cell of my body. *Baby Aldin.*

"Do you feel that, Aldin? Our son is communicating to us."

"I never thought I would ever have anything to call my own. When I met you, Wren, and what you represented to me, I knew my life would never be the same. And now, I have a son. *We* have a son. This moment is surreal. I only want two things in this world now. I want you. And, I want us."

Silence surrounds our moment in time. I can imagine a family coming together, and bathing in the happiness that comes with it.

"I also need to tell you that you come from an Enchanted Immortal lineage," he says. "You are from the Necromancer line. A powerful witch lives within you, waiting to emerge. Our joining has created our son and unlocked your magical side."

"Wait, what? You can't be serious." But honestly, even as I protest, I realize the truth behind his words. Deep in my soul, I feel the stirring of magic. "Okay, mister. I'm struggling here, but I do feel something big happening and have for a while. When I was a young girl, I realized that my dreams were sometimes a warning. I have this sixth sense about situations. I wasn't sure for a long time if it was a gift or a curse. Could this be part of what you're talking about?"

"Yes, my Wren. Your power is coming to the surface and one day soon you will learn to harness your special gift. You, my lovely Wren, will be an all-powerful witch."

"TMI alert. Haha! I guess we'll see if we ever get out of the fun house. Oh, shit! Shit! Shit! Sorry, baby Aldin. Before anything else, I have to tell you what I heard Baako say about the baby. He plans on taking our son's body for his own. He's a body snatcher, Aldin. We have to protect him, no matter the costs. I will not let them take him."

"You are fierce, my lovely. I will protect him. That, I can promise."

"One more thing. He's doing this all out of revenge for someone named Maarku. He longs to see him suffer."

"Maarku? Are you sure that's what he said?"

"Yes. He wants to take away everything he cares about. This guy or god or whatever he is, his elevator doesn't go all the way to the top, if you get my meaning." A warm feeling of going home floods my heart. "I feel like ... I feel it's time for you to go, Aldin. I don't want you to leave."

"Yes, my Wren. I feel it too. Be strong. Please don't give up. I will be coming for you and our son. Soon."

With his last words, Aldin's presence disappears, taking with him my hope. I'm alone again. Emotions of solace, comfort, and love surge through me. I realize I'm not alone anymore, and never will be again.

# CHAPTER

## 19

*Aldin*

When I come out of the Wren-induced trance, Marcus and the twins surround me, waiting for an update. I look into Marcus' eyes and know he was with me every second of the trip. He has the location to Baako's realm. Now all that is left is the opening of the doorway and I will be with her again.

"Baako is none the wiser. The baby is shielding our interaction. He has no idea we will be showing up on his doorstep later tonight."

Marcus nods. "I agree, Aldin. He is unaware. We have the element of surprise on our side."

"We need to find a weakness in the wards surrounding the doorway, something to break down the defenses so we can enter his domain," explains Jada, continuing to read from her spell book.

Hours pass by at a snail's pace. Marcus, Jazmine, and Jada have been tirelessly working on opening the doorway to Wren. Marcus receives emotions from my son through me. The bond between son and father is strong. I can feel his power growing steadily. He will be a force against the darkness we are fighting against. It shouldn't be long before they will be able to conjure a doorway to their location. Every minute they are within Baako's clutches is one too many for me.

A knock on the door surprises me. I hadn't heard the approach. Taking a deep breath, I inhale and respond, "Come on in, Fox."

The door opens and Brenton Fox saunters in. "The natives are restless, Kovac. What's the plan?"

Jada responds immediately, "You will be told when it is time, sir."

Brenton turns to her about to say something when Jazmine speaks. "Sister, you know the human is anxious. Please be patient."

Brenton's head goes back and forth, searching the twins. He's making me dizzy and I take pity on the man. "Agent Fox, this is Princess Jada and Princess Jazmine, known to everyone as the most powerful magical Immortal twins."

He extends his hand and, at the same time, the twins reach for him. The air in the room thickens and Jada snatches her hand away from him.

"Nice to meet you, ladies," he offers.

Jazmine hasn't moved. Her eyes are securely fastened on Brenton's face. A staring contest perhaps? Marcus comes back and sees what is taking place and I watch as his face clouds with anger. Thunder booms outside the windows and lightning flashes. A demonstration of his protective nature towards his sisters is being presented outside. A storm like no other has suddenly descended upon the city and I'm afraid until Fox releases Jazmine, it will continue.

"Remove your hand from the human now, dear sister, or I will be forced to remove his from his body," Marcus explodes.

The room goes silent.

I have witnessed Marcus angry many times, but never to the extent of what he is displaying towards Agent Fox. I'm concerned for his well-being and intervene on his behalf. "Fox, we need to gather the troops. I believe the doorway will be ready soon. Notify them to be ready for action. We are taking Jackson down."

He reluctantly releases Jazmine and turns to face me. "Are you sure you are ready for this after your blackout spell earlier?" asks Fox.

"I am more than ready. I have a million reasons to succeed and nothing will stop me from saving my true mate. Jackson has flaunted his depravity and sickness far too long. Tonight, we exterminate him from our world," I counter with a newfound confidence because of the bond I share with Wren and the life we have created.

"I will let them know we will be moving out soon." Fox replies. He glances in the direction of the twins, longing and interest covers his scared face. He salutes them as he walks out of the room.

The storm brewing outside subsides as the dribble of rain hits the glass windows. I peek a glance at Marcus. He is calming now. Slowly, the rain ends and a ray of sunshine filters into the room. I make my way closer to him. He is sitting in his prized chair, staring out the window at the skyline. Not one to always dwell on comforts, he allows himself one.

The corner of his lips raise, and I know my son is communicating with him now.

"Your blood is strong in the little one. His powers grow stronger by the minute," I mention to him.

"He is absorbing the knowledge required to help release Wren from the stasis Baako has her body in. He will need help from me to draw on his powers. He is learning quickly," Marcus notes.

Jada and Jazmine move from where they are sitting across the room and walk our way. "My brother, it is time. We have found a way in."

At their words, my heart soars at the prospect of holding Wren again. Not much longer, my love. I'm coming for you.

# CHAPTER 20

*Aldin*

We are all assembled in the foyer of the penthouse when Marcus and the twins appear in their royal ceremonial paraphernalia, clasping hands. The long white robes trimmed in gold accent the jeweled crowns upon their heads. Each is slightly different, representing the Enchanted Immortal races. The thrum of excitement and anticipation echoes off the walls. Few have witnessed the King and Princesses together in all their regal glory. Their power envelopes the crowded room waiting for instructions. Jazmine's eyes quickly glance Brenton's way and back before Marcus' deep voice captivates the audience.

"Aldin, once the doorway is open, Jada, Jazmine, and I will enter first. You will follow with the others. You will know when the time is right. Do not question yourself; allow your power to guide you. As for everyone gathered here, our mission is to retrieve Wren Bishop at all cost. She is more important than ending Jackson Parrish. She holds our future within her."

He does not wait for a response from me. His hand extends outward, the palm facing the floor, and moves his hand in a perfect circle. A bright light shimmers in the middle of the large foyer as the doorway to Wren appears. Stepping forward and united by their bonded hands, one at a time they enter the light—one moment here, the next transported to another realm.

I am momentarily dumbstruck with how my life has drastically changed in such a fleeting span of time. This time last week, the only priority I had was building Marcus' vast wealth and policing the rogues when necessary. Now, I have a true mate and a son on the way—something I never dreamed possible as an Enchanted Immortal. A calling forward touches me deeply, and I recognize the time is now.

"We enter now. Quietly, so as not to draw attention from Marcus."

I lead the Enchanted Immortals and Hunters

one at a time into the open doorway and what I see once I arrive startles me. Marcus and the twins stand in a semi-circle around Baako with Jafar at his back. There is an iridescent shield protecting them as Baako attacks using fireballs that changes colors as the fire is consumed by the shield.

"You cannot defeat me!" Baako screams wildly, releasing a large ball of fire towards the threesome.

"You cannot win, demented one. Only the righteous will prevail. We are more powerful than before and your time grows closer," Jada responds, only angering the beast more.

Jasmine taunts, "Your schemes have no power over us. I sense your terror, old one. How does it feel to know your end is near? Are you scared?"

"You always were the one that didn't know when to shut up. The favored one. Without them, you are powerless," Baako quips snidely.

Marcus remains eerily immobile during Jada and Jazmine's goading of Baako.

"Do not be afraid, little one. I am here." The words filter in my consciousness. Marcus is comforting my son and has opened a channel for me. "We are here to help release you and your mother. Where we go, no evil will follow. You will be safe."

I feel power radiating within me, and soon I am joined by two familiar beings. Three pieces meld into one: Marcus, my unborn son, and mine, a commanding force against evil. Light battling darkness.

Marcus directs the influx of power at Wren's imprisonment.

I hear him chanting and join in. "Shed not innocent blood, release thee from his power into the light."

The soft sound of chimes harmonize as we rhythmically repeat the phase over and over, opening the web holding Wren. At once, the gradual increase peaks and I'm thrown back into the present time alone.

My attention is torn away from the intense spell when I feel Wren's eyes on me, closing the gaping hole in my soul. She is awake. I become fully aware of that fact when a smile forms on her beautiful face, causing her eyes to sparkle with life. We have released her from being under Baako's spell.

I want her in my arms again where she belongs. I'm unsure now if I will be able to let her out of my sight once we are away from the danger here. Maybe years from now, I will allow her to venture from my side, but not before I'm ready.

We move towards each other. She is almost within my grasp when Jafar yanks her body back, stopping her forward progress. She kicks and pummels him with her fists, but her attempts don't phase the centuries-old Vampire. He is immune to her puny efforts. At her burst of anger, he lifts her off the floor and holds her closer.

"Let go of me, you big oaf! Gah, your breath is horrible," she squeals.

Jafar ignores her. He directs his loathing at me. "You are pitiful to think you could get away so easily with our vessel, young one. My liege has use of the unborn she carries."

I stop at his challenge, his words echoing in the pit of my stomach. Wren gazes at me. She is furious. I've got to get her away from him before she does something to anger him.

"Who do you think you are? Let go of my mate or suffer the consequences," I sneer, lacing the threat with all the pent-up anger I've held inside.

Movement behind Jafar catches my attention. Brenton is making his way closer to the Vampire. Jafar is preoccupied with his capture of Wren that he hasn't heard his approach. Jafar shifts forward as Brenton sinks the sharp hunting knife into his shoulder blade, causing him to drop Wren.

She runs into my open arms. The moment we reunite, I feel a surge of light within me.

But we are not yet safe. Hunters move in to protect Brenton from Jafar's wrath. I motion to Brenton to take Wren through the doorway to safety. I know she wants to stay, but her welfare comes first. "Go with Brenton and the others," I tell her. "Protect our son. We can talk about all this later, my Wren."

She nods, accepting my command. Brenton directs her to the doorway. First the Enchanted Immortals enter, then Wren, and the Hunters follow, protecting her at all costs.

Baako is engaged with Jada and Jazmine as Wren slips away. He only now realizes that Wren has departed his realm and is no longer under his spell. Baako erupts, sending balls of fire my way. With a wave of his hand, Marcus deflects the inferno into the walls beside him.

Marcus, who has remained silent until now, turns his wrath on Baako. "Stop playing like a child, Baako. If it wasn't for your selfishness, we would not be here. You are the reason we suffer now. Instead of enjoying our rich existence, you had to ripple the waters, changing the world to your liking. Why couldn't you have left them alone? They loved you unconditionally, yet you chose to use that love for evil. My promise to you, they will be found and returned. You cannot stop the chain of events that have begun. Choose your path wisely, my brother, or you will find yourself lost forever."

"So hopeful, Maarku," Baako sneers. "They are lost and your search will end up the same way it has over the last eight hundred years: empty and fruitless. As for your creation, I will use the baby as a vessel. You won't return my body, so I'll take his as mine. You lose either way."

I can no longer remain quiet. "I will never allow you near my son!"

Hideous laughter bounces off the walls, and a new doorway opens. Baako and Jafar walk into the light. Just as quickly as it appeared, the doorway vanishes and all traces of Baako with it.

A hand rests on my shoulder and I look up to find Marcus standing beside me. "Let's go home, Aldin. We live to fight another day. Your true mate awaits your return."

I walk into the light and waiting on the other side is my Wren. She wastes no time striding across the foyer and leaping into my outstretched arms.

"I love you, my Aldin. I don't want another minute to go by without you hearing it from me. I never want to lose you because my life has become more since you found me. I'd be lost without you. I love you."

"Ah, my lovely, feisty mate. Since the moment you came into my life, I knew you were the one I'd truly love 'til the end of time. My love for you is a journey starting at forever and ending at never. I love you too, my Wren."

She wraps her legs around my waist and her lips find mine. My Wren loves me. I'm minutes from ripping the jeans I am wearing from my body when a loud clearing of Marcus' throat has me refraining.

"I won't be available for a long, long time, my lord." I chuckle and smile at Wren. "We are going to talk among many other things, my Wren."

Laughter and well wishes are said as I make my way down the hall to my bedroom.

# CHAPTER 21

## *Wren*

We pause at the entrance of the stairwell inside the depths of the Great Pyramid in Egypt. Taking the steps in a single file line, the air becomes cooler and cooler as we descend. Glancing back, Aldin is watching me protectively, possessively. His face reveals his dominance, controlling my every step in his mind. Smiling to myself as I turn back around, I follow Marcus further into the recesses of the monolith, carefully taking each step because, duh, baby on board.

Today is our bonding ceremony. We will pledge ourselves to each other forever, which I'm committed to one hundred percent. It took me all of, what, a few days? Some things just happen that way. I can't deny the connection. Honestly, after all

**171**

that transpired, I no longer want to. Aldin explained that all bondings take place at the Temple of the Forever Living Immortal Scroll, a living entity within itself that keeps a log of all Enchanted Immortals where my name will be added next to his. The doorway is located in this pyramid, hence the reason we are in Egypt with our friends and family.

After our rescue, the events that followed caused my head to spin. I am *other*. I come from the Necromancer lineage on my mother's side of the family. I'm not a full-blown Enchanted Immortal yet, although the process has already begun. Yesterday I really wanted pickles and peanut butter and—*poof*, they appeared! I can get used to this. At first, it all seemed so unreal. I'm not into craziness, but I now understand.

And my life is beautiful. Complete.

Aldin is the other half to make me whole—the piece of my puzzle I didn't know I was missing until I met him. Not only that, but he has given me something I feared would never come to pass for me: my little baby Aldin. He's growing inside of me at a rapid rate, unlike a normal human pregnancy. From my calculations of his growth, I am well into my first trimester when it's only been a few weeks.

At this rate, baby Aldin will arrive in a little over three months. Awesome, right? Cutting my pregnancy down to a third of what a normal human pregnancy entails. Of course this is all speculation at best. Uncharted territory. I am the mother of an Immortal god. Try wrapping your head around that. But I couldn't be happier.

My mother is not nor has she ever been crazy. I am so grateful to the twins, Jazmine and Jada. They released my father from the bond my mother unknowingly cast upon his spirit when he died in the car accident.

*"Your mother has bound your father's spirit to her," Jada explains.*

*"She will not be made whole again until she frees him from this world, sending him to the realm of light," Jazmine finishes.*

*"We will help you, dearest sister of magic. Let us take this burden from her so she may live out her days in peace," the sisters relay in unison.*

*We gather hands around my mother's bed, connecting each of us. Mother, Jazmine, myself, and Jada—a perfect circle connecting us together as the chanting begins.*

*It is an emotional moment for my mother and*

*me. We both get to say goodbye to my daddy. He is set free, released of the bond to my mother and able to pass on into the light.*

A blessed day, that was. It was wonderful to bring mother home from the psychiatric hospital. We've had many question-and-answer sessions now that she's lucid again. I'll take it any day. She's going to live with us at the penthouse for now.

Marcus stops as we enter into the subterranean chamber lit by torches and decorated with gold and gems and hieroglyphs. At the far end of the room, a door-shaped structure illuminates the room, giving off the illusion of water, gurgling and swirling within it and beckoning for us to enter. Standing guard by the doorway are three Enchanted Immortals: a male Shifter, a male Vampire and a female Necromancer. Their races are distinguished only by the garments they wear, indicating them as sentinels protecting the doorway to the scroll.

As Marcus approaches, the three each take to a knee, bowing to their King in devotion.

Aldin grabs my hand, leaning down to whisper, "All is well, my Wren. Nothing can harm you or my son here."

So bossy. His son? Well, I'll give him that one,

today. He is my baby daddy. Besides, I love his dominant side. My nipples tighten and I squirm a little, pushing my legs together while trying to fend off my attraction for him.

Aldin's nostrils flare as he smirks with a knowing glance. I grasp his hand tighter while we walk through the liquid phosphorescence. An excited flutter begins within my belly. Emotions of love and coming home encompass me as we exit the brightness into another cavernous room.

The room fills with quiet reverence and gasps echo throughout. The humans in our bonding party grapple to comprehend what they see. Unlike the chamber in the pyramid, the room appears to be made of solid gold dotted by intricately placed gems of every precious-colored stone imaginable.

My eyes are drawn to the focal point in the room: a large scroll-like structure is erected in the center of the space, suspended from ceiling to floor and as tall as a two-story building. It is the Forever Living Immortal Scroll. As if it understands why we are here, the object glimmers. Delicately scripted crimson words appear on the living parchment. Aldin squeezes my hand and nods.

"My name, written down two hundred years ago. After the ceremony is complete, my Wren, yours will be added beside mine. You will be mine, forever. And one day when our son is born, his name will appear with ours." A smile radiates from his face and I grin back in return.

Comprehending the importance of this moment for us rests solidly within me—a forever binding of souls. Should one pass on, the other will follow. At one time, I would've been scared about the possibility, with the way my mother and father turned out. But the knowledge I've been gifted has changed my perspective. This is the way it should be.

I stare into Aldin's gorgeous dark orbs. Everything and everyone fades away. He is mine.

My Aldin coma is interrupted when I hear Marcus clear his throat and say, "We are ready to begin."

Marcus and the twins have moved to the front of the scroll, radiating affection, with Jada and Jazmine on each side of Marcus. All three are adorned with their ceremonial robes and crowns. Adoration flows freely from their faces.

Aldin and I move through the space to face them, the few friends and family parting as we walk by. Agent Brenton Fox, an old friend of Aldin's, stands with his gaze locked onto the front of the room. It seems he's watching the magical twins. Interesting. Next, I meet the tear-filled eyes of my mother. Candie is standing right next to her holding her hand with a matching expression.

I was so happy Marcus allowed me to share our story with her. When I brought Candie to the penthouse to meet everyone, there was a great disturbance in the force. *Ha!* The reaction Marcus and Candie had towards each other was bizarre at best. Marcus was polite but standoffish, and Candie was ... well, not Candie-like at all. She was snappy, pouty, and couldn't wait to leave. Totally weird in the Candie department. I haven't had the chance to talk to her about the whole encounter yet. *Note to self: Talk to Candie about her reaction to Marcus ASAP.*

Stopping in front of the trio, I turn to bask in the majestic man who, in just a few minutes, will be my bonded true mate—a blending of two souls deeper and more powerful than husband and wife. We're dressed in the ceremonial robes of bonding. The garments look more like togas with gold trim and sashes, identical except for the stone clasp that keeps everything together over the shoulder. Aldin's stone is blood red to represent the Enchanted Immortal Vampire race. A green stone adorns my robe in designation of the Enchanted Immortal Necromancer race.

Marcus begins to speak in the native tongue of Immortals—a beautiful otherworldly language. In this holy place, everyone can understand.

"We gather here in the Temple of the Immortal Scroll, the holiest of holies, anointed by the gods, to celebrate the joining of two souls. A true love pledge older than time and space. My son, Aldin Kovac, and the daughter of the matriarch Katrina, Wren Bishop."

The twins chime in, "Bonding to another, a true mate is not taken lightly."

Jada continues, "Two become one."

"Forever bound to the other," Jazmine follows as her eyes drift for a brief second behind me to where Brenton Fox is standing.

"Do you both come into this union of your own free will?" Marcus asks, looking to Aldin first.

"Yes, my lord. I love my Wren with everything that I am."

"Yes, my lord. I love this man, Aldin ... with everything that I am."

Marcus strides towards us holding out a golden ribbon. "The ribbon symbolizes the forever bond you are pledging before us. If this is a true match by the gods, it will radiate its approval for all here to witness."

With confidence, Aldin and I hold out our hands and Marcus begins to weave the ethereal sash around us, connecting us and tying it off at the end. The twins sing a celestial ceremonial verse behind him as he twines.

"Two become one. Forever bound to the other. The two halves become whole. Bonded forever."

Once the chanting stops, a tingle takes root. Electrical pulses tickle everywhere the ribbon touches my skin, beginning at the tips of my fingers. Aldin looks towards me, love and devotion captured on his face.

At the same time, the air thickens around me as the tingling from the twine becomes heated and cooled at the same time. Emotions of fulfillment, love, and unconditional service encircle me. As the bonding ribbon glows luminescent and diamond-like, I realize we are connected. Aldin, baby Aldin, and me ... together forever.

"The ribbon is bound and the bond is sealed. A true match created, pure and real." Marcus' cries of joy resound in the open room. The Immortal Scroll burns my name in the parchment underneath Aldin's, forever etched.

Cheers and applause erupt around us, yet all I see or feel is Aldin grabbing my face with his free hand as he devours my lips with his. My mate. Caught in our own little bubble, my happily ever after.

# CHAPTER 22

*Aldin*

I reach down and grasp Wren's neck with my unbound hand, pulling her close as I consume her lips with my parched mouth. Honey and heaven. My Wren. For a brief time, it is only the two of us standing in this holy place making love to each other with our mouths. The urge to consummate the bond prickles at my insides, coalescing at my dick as my fangs lower. I must have her soon.

Marcus' startled voice shakes me from my momentary lust.

"Sisters. Speak to me."

The twins are statue-still, gazing forward at nothing. Their eyes beaming opalescence rays. Brenton rushes forward to help and is blocked by Marcus' powerful arm.

"No! You will not pass."

"But something's wrong, Marcus. Let me help," Brenton expels in an aggravated tone.

"My son," Jada speaks in a strong, unearthly timbre.

Shocked by the voice of his sister, Marcus turns to look at the twins, side by side and holding hands.

"My son. I do not know how long we have before our spell is broken. Listen well."

Jazmine chimes in, "My precious little one. How we have missed you."

"Father. Mother. How is this possible?"

"The power of the bonding between these two remarkable individuals created the bridge for us to step through for a time. You now know that the prophecy is in motion and the first seal has been broken," Jada replies.

"Only the twins can find the talisman that will break the next seal. They alone hold the key to locate and unlock its power," Jazmine adds.

"I will help them on their quest, mother," Marcus concurs.

"NO!" Jada's powerful voice rocks the temple room. "You cannot leave! You must protect the child. Only a hunter can protect the twins. This hunter." Jada lifts her arm to point at Brenton Fox.

"What?" Marcus' booming tone brokers disgust and torment. "Not Fox, father. Anyone but him."

"It must be done, my son. It is our will." The twins speak in unison one more time before collapsing onto the hard stone floor.

Marcus and Fox rush towards the twins, concern and worry etched on their faces, and before they are able to reach them, they both stir. Jada nods at Marcus when he extends his hand to help her up. Fox helping Jazmine from the floor elicits a growl from Marcus. The closeknit group is shocked with the news and what will take place in the future.

Marcus turns in my direction. "My son, you are released, no longer bound to keep our secret. In light of everything that has happened here today, we are all connected and now know the truth of the situation. Our burden is great. The task ahead may be daunting, but we will succeed."

I nod in recognition and worry. His secret is out. Marcus knows he needs us all in the battle to come.

"Do not concern yourself, Aldin. This will be here upon your return. The doorway is opening and you must go. Enjoy the bonding time with your true mate, my son."

I clasp Wren's hand and step towards the light. "Thank you, father. I will see you when we return."

We enter the doorway to the other side to a realm Marcus chose especially for us to spend our bonding time. Wren's steps halt as she marvels at the natural beauty surrounding us. Crystallized stalagmites glowing a prism of colors dangle from the large cavernous area reflecting rays of light onto the sandy beach below. Water laps at the shoreline from an underground bubbling spring where a candlelit table set for two waits for us. I don't require food, but my Wren needs nourishment for the precious life she is carrying. Just off to the side of the table is a rock structure decorated with plush draperies inside containing luscious fabrics and pillows for her to rest on.

"Oh, Aldin! This is absolutely breathtaking. I don't think I've ever seen anything as beautiful in my entire life," Wren exclaims with excitement adorning her face.

I hold her close. The curves of her body fit mine, and I relish the idea she was made for me, only me. I see the sparkle in her eyes and for a moment I lose my train of thought. She is magnificent.

"My lovely Wren. Every day when you look in the mirror, the reflection you see is the most beautiful thing I have ever laid eyes on," I reverently utter.

Moisture forms in the corner of her blue eyes. Before she can continue, I sweep her into my arms and carry her towards the bed. When I reach the canopy, I place her on her feet and kiss the tip of her nose. Her arms twine around my neck, pulling me to her lips.

My fingers find the jeweled clasp on her shoulder, releasing the ceremonial robe to pool around her ankles and revealing creamy skin and nothing else. She steps towards me and the round bump in her midsection catches my attention. I bend to my knee, eye level and holding her stomach. I place wet kisses on the precious cargo she is carrying.

"Thank you for this miracle, my Wren."

"Aldin, you don't have to thank me for our son. He is ours."

I nod slightly, understanding that we created our miracle and the hope for the Enchanted Immortal race to help defeat Baako. Placing one last kiss on her tummy, I rise and unclasp the stone holding my robe in place. It falls to my feet and we are both standing as naked as the day we were born, admiring, wanting, and needing. Taking her hand, I lead her to the rich silky fabric.

We crawl towards the middle and lay down facing each other. My hand traces the angles of her face, arms, and tummy, memorizing the luscious feel of her soft body. I clasp her hand and lift it to my lips. "I'm going to love you forever, my Wren."

With a mischievous sparkle in her eyes, she says, "I'm so glad you passed my yummy test. Although, you were almost disqualified when you knew my name. Wasn't sure if you were a delusional sexy stalker, or my knight in shining armor," she says with a laugh.

"I'll show you 'sexy', my true mate."

Giving her a slight push, she lands flat on her back as I move my body in between her spread legs. *Heaven.* I place wet kisses down her neck, pausing where I marked her as mine. Licking, I scrape my teeth across the mark, eliciting a throaty moan from her. Her legs circle my hips and bump my throbbing shaft as she tries to satisfy the desire building inside her body.

"Not yet, my Wren. I'm going to sample and taste all of you ... every inch of your delicious body that belongs to me, worshiping my divine mate until you are begging me to come, wiping away all memories of the past, until your body, mind, and soul only know me as master, needing my touch to end your suffering."

"Oh, god! I mean ... yes, sir ... my Aldin," she utters in broken fragments.

Cupping her supple breasts, I tenderly suck and lap the rosy-pink tips, alternating back and forth, stirring her passion higher. My hand moves further down and locates the treasure I'm longing for and I insert my finger inside her center. When she twists, trying to escape the achy yearning I'm creating, I nip the tip of her breast with my teeth. Pain and pleasure bursts inside her and her vaginal muscles clench down like a vise on my finger.

"Hmmm, you like that, sweet Wren? Do you want more? Perhaps, my tongue inside your pussy?"

Moaning escapes from her as I inch lower, sampling her. I part the auburn curls hiding her weeping pink lips out of my way with my fingers. Next, I lower my mouth and relish the unique flavor of my true mate, lapping her musky entrance. I nuzzle her clit with my nose as she squirms, trying to break away from the hold I have on her. I insert my tongue in her pussy as her muscles squeeze, wanting more. I grind my aching dick into the sheets for some relief and almost come from the delectable woman I'm devouring. She's satisfying a need I was unaware I desired. I'll never want for more. My hands circle her ankles, opening her wider, bending her knees against the mattress.

Throaty groans of passion stream from her mouth. "Aldin … Don't stop …"

I know she's on the edge and won't last much longer. I find her pulsating nub, sucking it into my mouth. She tries to buck and grind her hips upwards when I secure my forearm across her body, restraining the movement. Holding her lower body firmly against the soft bed, I assert my strength and will over her. She succumbs to my dominance, once again fulfilling my needs with her actions.

Her body is primed and ready, blood filling her oversensitive clit. I bite and blood coats the inside of my mouth and down my throat as I continue to devour the life-sustaining blood my true mate is providing. Her screams echo throughout the cavern from the intense climax consuming her as I take what is mine. She is divine.

Still panting from the ecstasy I gave her, she

props herself on her elbows and looks down at me and smiles. "My turn, my Aldin."

Quickly, she catches me off-balance and I land flat on my back with Wren on her knees between my bent legs. She touches my ankles, then moves up my legs to my thighs. She bends and nips the dusty nipple on my chest before taking it into her mouth.

I growl. "You are playing with fire, my mate."

"Maybe, but I want to taste and learn what you like. Aren't you mine, too?" she hesitantly asks.

"Yes, I'm all yours, always. I long for your touch. I'm just not sure how long I can endure your exploration at the moment. I need to be inside you, my Wren, feeling your pussy gripping my cock as I thrust into you over and over."

"Oh, Aldin. You have such a sweet way with words," she says, her soft fingers lightly caressing my engorged staff. "You can't handle me touching you?" she challenges, then strokes my cock from root to tip.

The gauntlet is thrown and I readily accept. I lace my fingers at the back of my head, waiting to see what she has in store for me. She leans closer and I feel her hot breath near the tip of my weeping cock. The anticipation of feeling her lips around me causes a beastly growl from somewhere deep inside. Her eyes jerk up, ensnaring mine, a hint of amusement laced with desire. She lowers her lips and covers me with her warm, wet mouth. I know she won't be able to handle all of my girth, but she doesn't allow that to hinder her. No, my Wren wraps her hand around the base, pumping as she hollows her cheeks and creates a suction in rhythm. The intense pleasure overwhelms me and I'm about to lose my self-control. I tense, ready to grab her when she stops and, with a pop, lets my aching cock fall from her mouth.

"You taste so good, my Aldin," she taunts while continuing to stroke me. "Maybe you aren't as tough as you think, huh? Little ol' me has you right." Lick. "Where." Lick. "I want you." Lick.

Then, she covers the head of my cock with her mouth and swirls her tongue.

"Enough!" I roar and reach under her arms, lifting her body over me.

Her laughter filters through my lust-driven mind. I position her above my engorged cock and, with one thrust, I'm seated in her moist, tight pussy.

Her giggles turn to moans. Placing my hands on her hips, I demand, "Ride me, Wren."

She nods and positions her delicate hands on my chest. She raises herself on bent knees and tempts me with small strokes, only going past the head of my protruding member, not taking all of me. *Tease.* She's slowly building my desire until I can't think of anything else except wanting more of her—*all of her.* She stops and gradually lowers until her ass is resting on my thighs again. She tenses and squeezes her muscles, driving me crazy. She leans forward and my cock slips almost free of her tight channel as she thrusts down heavily on my shaft, grinding her hips at the end of the stroke and eliciting a cry of pleasure from me. I'm on fire and everywhere she touches ignites a new feeling. I can no longer resist the urge.

"Take from me. Drink my blood, Wren." My hand pulls her towards the spot between my neck and shoulder blade. "Make me yours, forever."

Holding her head gently, she wets the spot with her tongue using tiny swipes. Seconds later, the scrape of her canines against my skin has my dick twitching inside her. She strikes, sinking her newly formed fangs into my flesh and taking her first drink of me. Pleasure like nothing I have ever experienced in my long life swarms throughout me.

I encourage her. "Yes, that's it, love. Take all of

me." I don't want the moment to end.

She sucks, grinding her hips, and the small amount of restraint I had is gone. I'm no longer in control. I find her mark and bite, drawing her essence into my body. Her pussy clamps down even more. Grabbing her hips, I begin thrusting upwards and pulling her down on my shaft. She releases my shoulder and I retract my fangs from her. She lowers her mouth to mine and delves in, swiping her tongue against mine, tasting her essence. Ecstasy encompasses every movement. Together, we climb higher on the mountain of pleasure. In and out. Harder and harder.

"More, Aldin. I need more," she breathlessly screams.

Growling, I flip her onto her back and thrust deeper into her welcoming body. She meets me thrust for thrust, still searching for ultimate satisfaction.

"Fuck me, harder. Now," she demands.

I exit her body and roll her over.

"On your knees, Wren," I command panting.

She complies and I hunch over her back placing my hand to the side of hers. I grip my cock and enter her swiftly. Her quivering pussy lips clamp down and I'm lost to the pleasure she's providing as I power into her, stroke after stroke, deeper.

She releases a passionate scream as her womb holds me tighter, almost too painful to endure a moment more. I'm lost in pleasure as I erupt, streaming my hot cum into her.

Sometime later when our bodies cool and breathing returns to normal, I'm holding my precious mate, enjoying the time to reflect on how happy and complete she makes me.

"Did I really just grow fangs and drink your blood?" A giggle bubbles out of Wren.

Her laughter is contagious and I begin to chuckle. "Yes, my Wren. You're an Enchanted Immortal Necromancer. When you feed, your magic provides a way even without you knowing. Your body requires blood for nourishment, and because you're with child, your taste for food hasn't gone away. Does this change your feelings for me? For being my true mate?"

She gazes up at me with love and devotion and lays her hand over my heart. "I love you, Aldin. Forever."

Twirling a curl of her long hair around my index finger, I tell her, "A long time ago, a young boy wished for money, women, and immortality.

**193**

Not knowing what his heart truly desired. The folly of youth." I chuckle when she slaps my chest. "None of that compares to you, my Wren. Little did I know that my greatest wish would be wrapped up in a feisty, blue-eyed doctor. My wish came true the day I found you."

# EPILOGUE

## *Wren*

My life has been altered forever. I took a leave of absence from the hospital and that caused one chaotic mess. All of my patients were very understanding. It was the staff that didn't understand why I would leave. In the end, my mother was the excuse. I hated using her as a crutch but it seemed it was the only way to hide what was happening to me. She was glad to contribute after all the darkness she'd been through. Also, it would be hard to explain, "Oh, by the way, I'm carrying a god in my belly." Nope, no can do.

Baby Aldin is due any day now. We haven't picked a name yet, so until then, I'll use my nickname. I can't wait to hold him in my arms and count his fingers and toes. He's already smarter than the average womb baby. His emotions are getting stronger as he grows bigger. He sends thoughts in pictures, which blew my mind the first time it happened. Remarkable.

Aldin is perfect. Even with all of the doom and gloom happening around us, he never forgets to kiss me before he leaves or talks to our son via my belly. The link they share is amazing. Aldin always treats me like a princess, never taking anything for granted. Like I said: perfect. We still have a lot to overcome with Baako on the loose. The god of the night realm is one shady character wanting my baby's body for his own. No way that's ever going to happen as long as there is a breath left in me or my Aldin.

## *Aldin*

The future is uncertain for the Enchanted Immortals. Baako's unknown location and his desire for my son causes me to remain alert and ready for his attack at all times. The magical twins and Brenton Fox must obtain the sacred talisman in order to rid ourselves of him once and for all.

My newfound true mate helps ease the burden

I carry. She completes me. To think that everything which has happened to me over the centuries has been foretold ... a prophecy which involves me, my lovely Wren, our unborn godchild, Marcus, the twins, and Brenton Fox. We're stronger now as a whole, and because of that strength, we will win in the end.

Until that time comes, I will spend every waking moment enjoying my family. *My family.* Those two words hold such a powerful promise for me now. I still watch over my sister's descendants, but they are no longer the only reason for my existence. My Wren and our son ... they are mine. I no longer feel alone, never to be forgotten.

## *Jada & Jazmine*

We begin our journey to find the sacred talisman on the eve. Brenton Fox will be accompanying us and we are both joyful at the prospect of being one more step closer to unraveling the prophecy and returning Zenon and Augusta to the throne. Yet, Brenton causes a struggle to occur amongst ourselves. One of us wants nothing to do with him while the other relishes the idea of learning more about him.

Marcus has warned him away. Will he abide by his wishes or do what he wants? A yearning deep inside us longs for him, but to act on an emotion when we have more important issues to handle, must be buried and forgotten. For now, our quest is paramount.

### *Brenton*

Marcus' warning rings in my head. He scared the shit out of me. To put it mildly: me, hunter; him, god. His sisters are sacred. I am not to touch them. They are not mere mortals, but divine creatures on a quest for the talisman needed to end their evil brother. Wow, who would have thought Agent Brenton Fox would be assisting two goddesses on a divine quest? Certainly, not me.

I've noticed Jada is the mouthy one and Jazmine is the softer one. Both cause me to growl when other men approach, and when Marcus touches them, a sensation of ripping him to shreds overtakes me. I have no right to feel this way—and especially about two women, at that. I'm drawn not by their beauty alone, but their souls. I want to lap their pouty red lips and caress the silky skin underneath the robes they garner. A powerful tug of war is taking root. I want them both. How will this quest turn out? What does the future hold? Nobody knows ... not even me.

**Coming Next
in the Enchanted Immortals Trilogy:**

*Book 2: Fox's Awakening*

*Book 3: Marcus' Vengeance*

**Other books by F.G. Adams:**

*Grayson: Book 1, This is Our Life series*

*Keagan:  Book 2, This is Our Life series*
( Coming July 2016 )

Continue reading for a sneak peek of Keagan!

# ABOUT THE
## AUTHOR

F.G. Adams writes contemporary and paranormal romance about sexy alpha heroes and feisty-mouthed heroines. The wonder twins forming F.G. enjoy a healthy obsession of reading that started at a young age. Their books reflect an avid imagination that was cultivated by their grandmother who taught them the mind has no limits and to use both hands when reaching for the stars. Partners in writing, they both thrive on creating unique storylines for you, the reader, to enjoy.

When not writing, you can find them on a beach with their significant other enjoying the waves or riding a Harley on a country road somewhere in the USA.

Tell Us What You Think. Please leave a review. We enjoy hearing reader opinions about our books.

You can find us:

Website:    https://www.authorfgadams.com
Facebook:   https://www.facebook.com/AuthorFGAdams/
Goodreads:  https://www.goodreads.com/FGAdams
Twitter:    https://twitter.com/authorfgadams
Signup for Newsletter: http://eepurl.com/bRThVb
Pinterest:  https://www.pinterest.com/authorfgadams/

# AUTHOR'S NOTE

First, we would like to thank our husbands for their never-give-up attitudes. For understanding the endless days of take-out, dirty laundry and short-answer conversations while we write. Your ideas, suggestions, and never-ending support goes to show that happily-ever-after happens outside of a book. Thanks for being awesome!

Lesley, Michelle, and Erin, thank you so much for everything. We use those words because we would be writing another book with all that you do for us. Chance brought you ladies into our life and we so grateful to be able to call you our friends.

Feisty Flock...you ladies are amazing. Your support is truly appreciated and we love you, all! Thank you for your endless dedication in helping to share and support our books.

Thank you Daryl Banner for your editing and formatting expertise. As always you have a way with taking something great and making it even better. Thanks to Mayhem Cover Creations for bringing our vision to life and creating a spectacular cover.

To all the bloggers and readers: Thanks for taking a chance and reading our book. After all, we wouldn't be here without you!

xoxo
*F.G. Adams*

# KEAGAN

## *This is Our Life #2*

### Prologue

### *Jocelyn*

He's hurting her again. Her screams fill my ears even with the pillow covering my head. I'm cuddled on the full-size mattress with my little sister, Sage. We have the covers pulled over us hoping he won't see us if he tries to find us. Fallyn stepped in front of me when my dad was questioning me and took the blame for something I had done. She's my big sister and she runs interference between him and us all the time. It doesn't make sense. She baits him with her words until he doesn't see anyone else in the room but her. Now she was paying the price. It doesn't matter. If she wasn't here, it would be Sage, mother, or me. I really didn't mean to get her in trouble. I love her.

"Eighteen." The belt connects with flesh and Fallyn's voice is hoarse as she releases a cry of pain.

My father's voice continues counting. "Nineteen. Twenty."

Her screams have become whimpers and I know he's finished giving her twenty licks with his weapon of choice: the leather belt. I hate it. His belt symbolizes brutality and viciousness we are forced to live with daily. He had told her that if she didn't move and just took the lashes, then he wouldn't punish me too.

I hate him. He's evil.

"Go to your room and don't leave until you have my permission. You're not allowed out of this house for any reason." Dad continues his punishing instructions. "You won't be allowed to go to your slumber party this weekend, either."

I don't hear Fallyn reply and the bedroom door knob twists as the door opens. Fallyn gently walks to the bed and starts climbing up on the mattress. We part, allowing her to crawl between us to lie down. We carefully surround her and hold her hands, not touching anywhere else.

"Are you okay, Fallyn?" Sage whispers.

She sniffles and faintly replies, "Yes."

"Do you want a drink? I can sneak out and get you something," I offer, my conscience wrestling with blame and sorrow after what she endured.

"No," she replies, shaking her head. "He would catch you."

"Do you still love me, Fallyn?" I ask her, scared of what her answer will be.

"I'll always love you, both of you. What happened wasn't your fault, Jo. It's his. We have each other and no matter what, that's never gonna change. Remember, we're the three musketeers. One for all and all for one, right?"

We both reply, "Yes."

"I love you, Fallyn."

She's drifting off to sleep and I know we have to stick together. I'm only five years old, but I've stayed at my Aunt Polly Jean's house and their family isn't like ours. Her husband doesn't whip his daughters like my dad does. I wish he would be nice. Every child deserves good parents and not every parent deserves a child; unfortunately for me and my sisters, my dad has three daughters.

# CHAPTER 1

*Ten years later*

## *Keagan*

It's my first day of high school as a junior and I don't know a soul. My parents serve in the military and we've moved so many times, I've lost count. We moved to Lakeview, Florida this summer when my dad received new orders. They have served in the Air Force all my life.

I walk into the first class and I'm greeted by stares. New kid on the block. I don't stop until I've reached the back corner and slide into the chair. Glancing up, my stare returns to the door when a group of kids make their way in and take their seats in chairs next me.

"Hey dude, you new to the area?" the biggest one of the group of guys asks.

I shrug. "My family moved here in July."

"What's your name?" he inquires.

"Keagan."

He smiles and salutes me. "I'm Bo, and that's David. He's a transplant, too. I've lived here all my life and David moved here last spring. This place is cliquish and if you weren't born here, it's hard to make friends. So stick with us and we'll show you the ropes."

We are interrupted when the door opens and laughing echoes in the room. I look up and see her. She's taller than the girl walking beside her, but you can see the similarities. They are related.

She's an angel and I want to know who she is.

"That's the Blackwood sisters. They're off-limits, so don't even waste your time. Totally out of your league," Bo comments when he notices me staring.

David nods and adds, "Their dad owns most of the town. He has a big ranch near Pond Creek. Couple of guys got busted out there a few weeks back and he tackled 'em and called the cops. They were trying to sneak and meet with Fallyn. She's the shorter one."

I continue to stare. "Who's the other one? What's her name?"

"Jocelyn. She's really shy and doesn't talk to anybody but her sister. She comes to school, cheers, and goes home. That's about it."

"Why's that?"

"Not sure. She keeps to herself."

Our conversation ends when the bell rings. The teacher stands and begins the lesson. I want to know more about the angel named Jocelyn.

## Jocelyn

I finally get to attend school with Fallyn. It's my first day of high school and I'm really nervous, but just like always, Fallyn is teaching me what I need to know and hasn't left my side except to go to her classes. She's in the last class of the day—art—and we are on our way there.

"How's your first day going? You haven't had any problems, have you? You'd tell me if someone picked on you, right?" Fallyn interrogates me as we walk.

"No. I haven't spoken to anyone today at all."

"Why the hell not, Jo? You don't have to blend here. You can make friends. I'll protect you."

"Just don't want to."

"Okay, sis. We're almost done and then I've got practice. How 'bout you?"

"Not today, but I think I'll wait for you in the gym. That way, we can leave together."

"You know, you're looking really good in those boots, JoJo. I can't believe you actually wore 'em to school."

"Why the heck not? They totally rock this skirt, and you know I love my pink snakeskin boots."

"That's the prob, sis. It's the 80's, for God's sake! I'm wearing jeans and converses and you've got your boots. We are *so* opposites in clothing."

We both start giggling as we walk into the classroom. Everybody stops and stares at us. I know Fallyn likes the attention, but I prefer not to be seen. I want to remain in the background. It's been an instinctive action since I can remember. I'm able to keep him from attacking me if he doesn't see me. There's been many times that Fallyn hasn't been home and I've been in his path.

"Where do you wanna sit?" I look back at her and she's grinning.

"Follow me."

"Why do I feel like you're about to embarrass me?"

"No clue, Jo," Fallyn replies and weaves in and out of the desks until she stops in front of a guy I've never seen around here before. She puts her backpack down on the desk and slides into the chair. I follow suit and sit down beside her, wondering why in the world she chose to sit so far back in the room.

"Don't look now, but you've got an admirer," she whispers when Mrs. Campbell begins calling attendance.

"Huh? What're you talking about, Fallyn?"

"Someone couldn't take their eyes off you as we were walking around looking for a seat. I'm just trying to help my little virgin sister get a date," she adds with a smirk.

"Fallyn! Good grief. Don't do me any favors. Please!" I beg.

We quiet when Mrs. Campbell's stern glare turns our way. When the bell rings and class is over, I make for the exit only to be stopped by Fallyn when she grabs my arm and loops hers with mine, slowing my progress.

"What's the rush? Aren't you curious?"

"No. Not at all. I want to leave."

"Come on, sis. Live a little."

I'm stuck. She won't let this go until I give in, so I nod, and she eagerly stops us and waits for their group to catch up.

"What's up?" Bo asks as he hugs Fallyn.

"Hi, Bo. Who's your new friend?" Fallyn asks with a smile.

"Keagan. Sorry man, didn't get your last name."

"Keagan Fontneau," the boy answers. "Just moved here from Texas. Nice to meet y'all," he says, smiling at me.

I don't say anything and lower my eyes.

"Well, okie dokie. I've got practice. Let's go, Jo."

I look up and he's staring at me with a stony expression on his face. He's got the most beautiful blue eyes I've ever seen. I'm jerked from the moment as Fallyn pulls me away and into the hall.

What in the world was that? I never look at guys, and I'm positive he's totally not interested in me.

Did you enjoy this sneak peek?

Be looking for
*Keagan: This is Our Life #2*
coming July 2016.

Made in the USA
Charleston, SC
08 September 2016